Samuel French Acting Edition

Johnny Manhattan

Book and Lyrics by
Robert Lorick

Music by
Dan Goggin

‖SAMUEL FRENCH‖

SAMUELFRENCH.COM   SAMUELFRENCH.CO.UK

FOR PRODUCTION ENQUIRIES

UNITED STATES AND CANADA
Info@SamuelFrench.com
1-866-598-8449

UNITED KINGDOM AND EUROPE
Plays@SamuelFrench.co.uk
020-7255-4302

Each title is subject to availability from Samuel French, depending upon country of performance. Please be aware that *JOHNNY MANHATTAN* may not be licensed by Samuel French in your territory. Professional and amateur producers should contact the nearest Samuel French office or licensing partner to verify availability.

MUSIC USE NOTE

Licensees are solely responsible for obtaining formal written permission from copyright owners to use copyrighted music in the performance of this play and are strongly cautioned to do so. If no such permission is obtained by the licensee, then the licensee must use only original music that the licensee owns and controls. Licensees are solely responsible and liable for all music clearances and shall indemnify the copyright owners of the play(s) and their licensing agent, Samuel French, against any costs, expenses, losses and liabilities arising from the use of music by licensees. Please contact the appropriate music licensing authority in your territory for the rights to any incidental music.

IMPORTANT BILLING AND CREDIT REQUIREMENTS

If you have obtained performance rights to this title, please refer to your licensing agreement for important billing and credit requirements.

JOHNNY MANHATTAN had its world premiere at Meadow Brook Theatre (Cheryl L. Marshall, Managing Director; Travis W. Walter, Artistic Director), in association with Lyle Saunders, in Rochester Hills, Michigan, on September 9, 2017. The performance was directed and choreographed by Mark Martino, with sets by Brian Kessler, costumes by Liz Goodall, lighting by Matthew J. Fick, and sound by Michael Duncan. The Production Stage Manager was Terry W. Carpenter, and the Music Director was Michael Rice. The cast (in order of appearance) was as follows:

LORRAINE	Lauren Sprague
MAXIE	Ruth Pferdehirt
GLORIA	Alissabeth Morton
FRANCINE	Janet Caine
MICKEY	Nathan Cockroft
GARY	Tyrick Wiltez Jones
JOHNNY	Jim Ballard
ROSIE	Anne Brummel
DOROTHY	Barbara McCulloh
DAVID	George Dvorsky
RITA	Jana Robbins
EDWARD	Scott Willis
GEORGE	Ian Turnwald
PAUL	Dale White

CHARACTERS

JOHNNY – The Club Owner. Very handsome, debonnaire. In his early 40's. Tenor or high baritone, dancer.

ROSIE – The Lady on the Piano. Very attractive, 30–40. Excellent singer with a wide range, moves well. Was Johnny's former girlfriend.

DAVID DARLING – Johnny's lawyer. A suave Connecticut success story, 40–50. Baritone, some dancing. He is having an affair with Lorraine.

DOROTHY DARLING – David's wife. A very elegant and regal "Connecticut wife." 40–50. Legit soprano, some dancing.

RITA – An Actress. A "Norma Desmond" type. A fading star, 65-ish. Strong singer with a good belt range.

EDWARD – A Writer. Charming and elegant but past his prime as a writer. 55–65. High Baritone, Good dancer.

LORRAINE – A Showgirl. The club's featured singer, 25–35. Jazz singer with wide range. Dancer. She is having an affair with David.

MAXIE – A Showgirl. One of the showgirls who feels her talent has been overlooked by Johnny. 30–40. Strong belt voice with some legit. Has a tour-de-force eleven o'clock number. Dancer.

MICKEY – The Escort. Rita's escort. More handsome than smart. 25–40. Baritone, some dancing.

GLORIA – A Showgirl. Good singer and dancer. 25–30.

FRANCINE – A Showgirl. Good singer and dancer. 25–30.

GARY – The Bartender. Baritone/tenor. Dancer. 25–30.

PAUL – A Waiter. Baritone/tenor. Dancer. 25–30.

GEORGE – A Waiter. Baritone/tenor. Dancer. 25–30.

SETTING

"One more night in Manhattan" at Johnny's nightclub.

It's November 1958 when clubs like the Copacabana and El Morocco were filled with socialites and glamorous entertainers.

MUSICAL NUMBERS

ACT ONE

At Johnny Manhattan's/For Old Times' Sake . . . . .Johnny, Rosie,
Mickey, Gary, Lorraine, Maxie,
Francine, Gloria, George, and Paul
Anonymous Town . . . . Company
Bits and Pieces . . . . Johnny and Company
For Better or For Worse . . . . David and Dorothy
She Takes Very Good Care of Herself. . . . . Mickey, Gary,
Paul, and George
Luxury. . . . . Rita and Edward
I'll Sing Your Favorite Song . . . . .Rosie
Johnny's Girls/A Continental Guy . . . . .Johnny, Francine, Gloria,
Maxie, and Lorraine
Morning Man . . . . Lorraine, Gloria, and Francine
Remarkable. . . . . David, Dorothy, Rita, Mickey,
Lorraine, Maxie, Gloria, and Francine
New York is Driving Me Crazy. . . . . .Johnny, Rosie, and Company

ACT TWO

New York is Driving Me Crazy (Reprise). . . . . Johnny and Company
Where in the World is the World That I Wanted?. . . . . .Johnny
Quiet, Intimate, Little Restaurants. . . . . .Rosie
Oh, Those Johnnies. . . . . .Rita
I Don't Do That Anymore . . . . Edward
Mister Producer . . . . Maxie
And I Would Go Away . . . . Dorothy
Every Now and Then. . . . . David
For Old Times' Sake (Reprise). . . . . .Rosie and Johnny

ACT ONE

[MUSIC NO. 1 "AT JOHNNY MANHATTAN'S"]

(Lights up on **GLORIA, MAXIE, FRANCINE** *and* **LORRAINE.** *They're working on a dance routine.* **GARY** *is behind the bar.* **GEORGE** *and* **PAUL** *are in and out arranging things.)*

LORRAINE. Oh, I'll never get this step.

MAXIE. No, you probably won't.

LORRAINE. Aren't you gonna warm up?

MAXIE. I already did...last year.

GLORIA. I don't suppose there'll be many people here tonight.

LORRAINE. Johnny said a small private party.

FRANCINE. Same amount of work. So what's the difference.

MAXIE. I heard something interesting.

LORRAINE. That's unusual.

GLORIA. Maxie, don't start.

MAXIE. I heard a certain regular customer will be coming in tonight.

LORRAINE. Oh?

GLORIA. Please don't start, Maxie.

MAXIE. And he's bringing a special guest.

GLORIA. Maxie!!

MAXIE. Look, I don't want to start any trouble. I just heard the guy is bringing his wife, that's all. I just wanted to warn you, Lorraine.

LORRAINE. I know all about it. Thanks, anyway. I think you could use a little more mascara, dear. I can still see your eyes.

GIRLS.

> AT JOHNNY MANHATTAN'S ON FIFTY-THIRD STREET
> WE NEVER QUIT TILL DAWN.
> THE REST OF NEW YORK GETS READY FOR WORK
> AND WE'RE STILL CARRYING ON AND ON AND ON AND
>   ON...

LORRAINE. What was that step?

MAXIE. Oh, don't worry honey. It would take all year. C'mon girls, let's change.

> (**MAXIE** *and* **FRANCINE** *exit.* **LORRAINE** *and* **GLORIA** *continue talking.* **MICKEY** *enters from the club entrance.*)

LORRAINE. *What* is her *problem?*

GLORIA. She's got no man. Her career's going nowhere. It's kinda sad.

> (*They exit.*)

MICKEY. Who's the guest of honor?

GARY. Johnny is. How come you're all dressed up. Mickey?

MICKEY. Oh Johnny put me on escort duty. Someone's grandmother no doubt.

> (**MICKEY** *exits to put his coat away.* **JOHNNY** *enters.* **CHORUS GIRLS** *and* **WAITERS** *go in and out casually through the scene but staying "out of the focus.")*

JOHNNY.

> ONE MORE NIGHT IN MANHATTAN
> ONE MORE NIGHT IN NEW YORK
> ONE MORE RIVER OF CHAMPAGNE

GARY.

> ALL THESE BOTTLES TO UNCORK.

JOHNNY.

> ONE MORE NIGHT IN THE CITY
> ONE MORE NIGHT WITHOUT A BREAK.
> BUT A RIVER OF CHAMPAGNE
> MAKES IT EASIER TO TAKE
> FOR OLD TIMES' SAKE.

But tonight it'll be different Gary. They're all coming. I must be out of my mind.

GARY. I just hope they all get along. Is that why you've been so edgy lately?

JOHNNY. Well, I'm just trying to put the pieces of this particular puzzle together.

GARY. Sounds serious, Johnny.

JOHNNY. Oh yes, there's big news tonight, Gary.

> (ROSIE *enters unnoticed by* JOHNNY *and* GARY. MAXIE *gives her a hug.* ROSIE *goes up and sits on the piano.*)

ARE THE PIECES OF MY PAST
STRONG ENOUGH TO STAND THE QUAKE?
DOES LOVE DIE OR DOES IT LAST
FOR OLD TIMES' SAKE?

SHALL I OFFER THEM THE CHOICES
THEY NEVER OFFERED ME?
SHALL I LISTEN TO THE VOICES...

ROSIE.

JOHNNY, JOHNNY,
ALL NIGHT THROUGH.
EV'RYTHING REMINDS ME
OF YOU...

> (*Underscoring continues.*)

JOHNNY. Rosie. You look great. "The Lady on the piano!" Right where you belong. I haven't seen you since...

ROSIE. Since you didn't marry me.

JOHNNY. Forgive me?

ROSIE. Why not? Everybody else has. Hi, Gary!

GARY. Nice to see you back, Rosie.

ROSIE. Well, Johnny, what's up? Why the telegram? It sounded so urgent.

JOHNNY. I'm throwing a party. A private, intimate, urgent party. But no questions.

ROSIE. Not even who's invited?

JOHNNY. Old friends. You. Rita.

ROSIE. I guess that means she's still alive.

JOHNNY. Edward.

ROSIE. Wasn't he Rita's husband?

JOHNNY. Yes. They haven't seen each other in years but I've kept up with both of them. David's coming. You remember. My lawyer. My best friend.

ROSIE. So who else?

JOHNNY. Just the staff.

ROSIE. Lovers?

JOHNNY. There hasn't been anyone.

ROSIE. You've changed, Johnny. More of a devil, I'd say.

JOHNNY. Blame it on the city.

ROSIE. Blame it on your ass! You and your awkward situations.

JOHNNY. Give me half a reason and I'll leave right now.

ROSIE. What? And miss the fun?

> *(By this time the entire staff should be in various areas of the stage.)*

[MUSIC NO. 1A "FOR OLD TIMES' SAKE"]

FOR OLD TIMES' SAKE WE'LL SPEND
ONE MORE NIGHT IN MANHATTAN
ONE MORE NIGHT IN NEW YORK
ONE MORE RIVER OF CHAMPAGNE

GARY.

ALL THOSE BOTTLES TO UNCORK.

JOHNNY, ROSIE, GARY, GEORGE, PAUL, MICKEY LORRAINE, MAXIE, FRANCINE & GLORIA.

ONE MORE NIGHT IN THE CITY,
ONE MORE NIGHT WITHOUT A BREAK
BUT A RIVER OF CHAMPAGNE
MAKES IT EASIER TO TAKE

JOHNNY.

SHALL I TAKE THEM ON A TEAR?
SHALL I LET DEFENSES FALL?

SHALL I TRY TO CLEAR THE AIR
FOR ONCE AND FOR ALL

ALL TEN.

FOR OLD TIMES' SAKE?

ROSIE.

GARY, CHILL THE BEST CHAMPAGNE.

GARY.

LET'S SNIFF SOME COCAINE.

ROSIE.

LET'S DECORATE A CAKE.

JOHNNY.

DECORATE A CAKE.

ROSIE.

LET'S ORDER UP SOME RAIN

JOHNNY & GARY.

ORDER UP SOME RAIN.

ALL TEN.

FOR OLD TIMES' SAKE.

ROSIE.

FINGERS CROSSED
GIVE YOUR WORLD A SHAKE.

JOHNNY. I don't think I know who these people are anymore.

ROSIE & GARY.

WELL, PRETEND THAT YOU DO
FOR OLD TIMES' SAKE.

ALL TEN.

FOR OLD TIMES' SAKE.

[MUSIC NO. 2: "ANONYMOUS TOWN"]

(Intro starts immediately as **GARY** *throws the main switch. Lights come up on the entire club revealing it for the first time.* **DAVID, DOROTHY,** *and* **RITA** *enter.* **EDWARD** *enters a few beats later alone and is not noticed by* **RITA.**)*

(There is general chatter leading into:)

LORRAINE.

HAVE WE MET?

MAXIE.

HAVE WE MET?

ROSIE.

HAVE WE MET?

GLORIA & GEORGE.

HAVE WE MET?

GARY.

DID I MEET YOU AT THE VANDERBILTS' PARTY?

PAUL.

OR WAS IT AT THE GOVERNOR'S BALL?

ROSIE.

YOU RAN WITH THAT CROWD THAT WAS SO TERRIBLY
ARTY.

THINGS HAVEN'T CHANGED AT ALL.

LORRAINE.

DID I MEET YOU IN SUN VALLEY?

WERE WE COZY IN SOME CHALET?

PAUL.

DO YOU HAVE A STRANGE ATTRACTION TO JAZZ?

DOROTHY.

PERHAPS IT WAS THE BALLET?

RITA.

PEACOCK ALLEY?

MICKEY.

I'LL LAY YA TEN TO ONE IT WAS THE BATHS.

GIRLS.

DID I MEET YOU AT THE PLAZA OR WAS IT TRADER VIC'S?

YOU KNOW IT'S AWF'LLY HARD TO TELL.

GUYS.

THE FACE IS FAMILIAR, THE NAME SORT OF CLICKS

AND THE BODY RINGS A BELL.

ALL.

NEW YORK, NEW YORK. ANONYMOUS TOWN.

THE INVITATION READS "KINDLY ATTEND".

GIRLS.

JUST CAN'T REFUSE IT. MUST MEET WHO'S-IT.
AND WHAT'S-HIS-NAME IS MY BEST FRIEND!

ALL.

NEW YORK, NEW YORK. ANONYMOUS TOWN.

GUYS.

SHADY LADIES IN ERMINE AND FOX.
GIVE ME GIRLS IN SATIN, WE'LL FLATTEN MANHATTAN.

ALL.

MANHATTAN ON THE ROCKS.

GARY.

WAS IT THE NIGHT THAT POOR TALLULAH
GOT SO TIGHT SHE DID THE HULA

PAUL.

AND GERTIE TRIED TO DANCE,
BUT COULDN'T QUITE?

FRANCINE.

THERE WAS ALFRED.

MAXIE.

THERE WAS LYNN.

RITA.

THEY LET JUST ANYBODY IN!

ROSIE.

AND LILY PONS SANG "QUEEN OF THE NIGHT."

DAVID.

WERE WE FIGHTING THE ENNUI
OVER SAUTÉED JAMBE DE GRENOUILLE?

DOROTHY.

IN CASE YOU DON'T KNOW FRENCH,
MY DEAR, THAT'S FROGS.

RITA.

WERE WE SHEDDING EXTRA POUNDS
RIDING TO THE HOUNDS?

GARY.

I THINK SHE MEANS
"WE'RE GOING TO THE DOGS."

GIRLS.

OH, NO!

ALL.

NEW YORK, NEW YORK. ANONYMOUS TOWN.
THEY'RE BOUND TO FORGET YOU ON SIGHT.
SAVOR EACH TRUFFLE, GET LOST IN THE SHUFFLE
AND FIGHT, FIGHT, FIGHT THE GOOD FIGHT.
RAH! RAH! RAH!

(Dance break.)

GIVE ME GIRLS IN SATIN, WE'LL FLATTEN MANHATTAN,
MANHATTAN ON THE...

GIRLS.	**GUYS.**
ROCKS!	NEW YORK, NEW YORK
NEW	NEW YORK, NEW YORK
YORK	NEW YORK, NEW YORK

GIRLS & GUYS.

NEW YORK!

[MUSIC NO. 2A "COCKTAIL MUSIC"]

(Everyone is talking, laughing. **JOHNNY** *takes in the scene.)*

RITA. Oh, Johnny you think of everything. *(To* **MICKEY.***)* What is your name, dear?

MICKEY. Mickey.

RITA. Johnny, you have slipped me a Mickey. We'll talk. Later.

JOHNNY. Yes.

EDWARD Gonna do some tricks for us tonight, Johnny?

JOHNNY. Sure.

EDWARD She hasn't recognized me yet.

JOHNNY. She will.

*(***GARY** *goes to the Darlings' table.* **JOHNNY** *crosses to them slowly.)*

GARY. Can I get you something?

DAVID. The usual. I mean... I...usually have Scotch. But... tonight feels like champagne, doesn't it?

DOROTHY. *(To* **GARY.***)* Why don't you just bring a case to the table then he won't have to bother you again? Johnny can afford it, can't you Johnny?

JOHNNY. Sure. Have whatever you want.

> (**GEORGE** *brings a bottle of champagne and glasses.*)

GARY. I'll be at the bar if you need me.

DAVID. We won't.

> *("Cocktail Music" fades out.)*

DOROTHY. I might. Johnny, it's nice to see you. The boys ask for you all the time.

JOHNNY. I'm sorry I haven't been over.

DAVID. We've all been very busy.

DOROTHY. Very busy. I love your club, Johnny. David's always refused to bring me because he thought I wouldn't. It's charming.

[MUSIC NO. 3 "BITS AND PIECES"]

JOHNNY. Well, I'm glad you're here. Both of you.

> (**JOHNNY** *sings in a single spotlight. The others don't hear him. The song is his private thought.*)

BITS AND PIECES OF A LIFE.
GATHERED HERE, BUT WHY TONIGHT?
I KEEP STUBBING MY TOE ON YESTERDAY,
BANGING MY HEAD AGAINST TOMORROW.
ISN'T IT FUNNY HOW EVERYTHING STAYS THE SAME?

BITS AND PIECES OF THE DREAM,
COME AND GO. HOW STRANGE IT SEEMS.
WHO IS THAT LADY ON THE PIANO?
WHO IS THAT MAN AT A CORNER TABLE?
ISN'T IT FUNNY HOW EVERYTHING CHANGES? ...CHANGES.

JOHNNY.
> WHERE CAN I REST MY HEAD?
> WHO HAS THE SOFTEST SHOULDER?
> WHO'S SLEEPING IN MY BED?
> JOHNNY, ARE YOU GETTING OLDER?

ALL BUT JOHNNY. *(In low light as if they are ghosts haunting* **JOHNNY,** *gradually getting louder each time.)*
> OLDER.

JOHNNY.
> OLDER?

ALL BUT JOHNNY.
> OLDER.

JOHNNY.
> OLDER?

ALL BUT JOHNNY.
> OLDER!

JOHNNY.
> BITS AND PIECES OF TIME
> FILLING THE ROOM AND ISN'T IT FUNNY
> I KEEP STUBBING MY TOE ON YESTERDAY,
> BANGING MY HEAD AGAINST TOMORROW.
> ISN'T IT FUNNY HOW NOTHING CHANGES
> AND NOTHING IS EVER THE SAME?
> ISN'T IT FUNNY, ISN'T IT FUNNY,
> ISN'T IT FUNNY HOW NOTHING IS EVER THE SAME?

[MUSIC NO. 3A "COCKTAIL MUSIC"]

*(**LORRAINE** crosses to **JOHNNY**.)*

LORRAINE. Johnny! I'd like to dance.

JOHNNY. Lorraine, do you know Mr. and Mrs. Darling?

> *(Note:* **LORRAINE** *and* **DAVID** *are having an affair.* **JOHNNY** *knows this.* **DOROTHY** *doesn't, but is suspicious.)*

DOROTHY. How do you do?

LORRAINE. Hello.

JOHNNY. Lorraine works for me.

DOROTHY. What do you do?

LORRAINE. A little bit of everything.

> (**LORRAINE** *gives* **DAVID** *a look.*)

DOROTHY. Sweet.

LORRAINE. C'mon Johnny, I wanna dance. Isn't it refreshing to see the nouveau riche exercising a little noblesse oblige.

JOHNNY. Ah, Lorraine. You've been taking French lessons I see. Shut up and dance.

> (*They dance off in the darkness. Lights up on* **DAVID** *and* **DOROTHY.**)

DOROTHY. Something's up.

DAVID. What?

DOROTHY. I don't like the way that girl was looking at you.

DAVID. I didn't notice. Dorothy, let's try to have a good time tonight.

DOROTHY. It's been a long time since we were out together. It seems the more money you make, the less I see you. Are we very rich, David?

> (*"Cocktail Music" fades out.*)

DAVID. Yes. I'm afraid so.

DOROTHY. You weren't home before eleven once last week.

DAVID. Next week we'll spend an evening together...at home... Just the two of us.

DOROTHY. We did that once. Remember? Please don't be nice to me David. It's easier that way. And if things are going to be difficult between us, at least they should be easy.

[MUSIC NO. 4 "FOR BETTER OR FOR WORSE"]

DAVID. You're amazing.

DOROTHY. You're not.

> A BREAKFAST COMPANION,
> IS THAT ALL YOU ARE?
> I WARM UP THE COFFEE
> YOU WARM UP THE CAR.
> AND NOTHING ELSE!
> YOU'RE SOMEONE TO ZIPPER
> THE BACK OF MY DRESS.

DAVID.

> BUT LATELY...

DOROTHY.

> WHAT?

DAVID.

> NOTHING!

DOROTHY.

> NO, SAY IT.

DAVID.

> NO! GUESS!

DOROTHY. Look, if you're implying that I'm gaining weight, it's probably because I don't get very much exercise.

DAVID. You stopped being available.

> A DINNER COMPANION,
> IS THAT ALL YOU ARE?
> I CALL 'CROSS A CANYON
> "TRY THE CAVIAR,

> It's delicious."

DOROTHY.

> A DINNER COMPANION
> NO, NOT EVEN THAT.
> I GET MORE COMPANIONSHIP
> FROM THE CAT!

> And we don't even have a cat. I know. They make you sneeze. That ridiculous sneeze!

BOTH.

> TWO INDIVIDUAL HEADS.
> TWO INDIVIDUAL TOMBS.

THIS YEAR SEP'RATE BEDS.
NEXT YEAR SEP'RATE ROOMS!

DAVID.

I MARRIED YOU FOR BETTER OR FOR WORSE.

DOROTHY.

AM I THE VICTIM OF SOME EVIL CURSE?

BOTH.

THE BETTER THINGS HAVE ALL GONE BY THE WAYSIDE
THE WORSE THINGS HAVE ALL GOTTEN WORSE.
I MARRIED YOU FOR ALL THE THINGS
I'D ONLY FOUND IN YOU.
NOW I WISH I COULD REMEMBER ONE OR TWO

INDIVIDUAL MINDS
BOTH SPOUTING YESTERDAY'S NEWS.
THIS YEAR UNDOUBTEDLY FINDS
WHAT NEXT YEAR WILL CERTAINLY LOSE.

DOROTHY.

I MARRIED YOU FOR BETTER OR FOR WORSE.

DAVID.

AM I THE VICTIM OF SOME EVIL CURSE?

BOTH.

THE BETTER THINGS HAVE ALL GONE BY THE WAYSIDE.
THE WORSE THINGS HAVE ALL GOTTEN WORSE.
I MARRIED YOU FOR ALL THE THINGS
THAT I'D ONLY FOUND IN YOU.
NOW I WISH I COULD REMEMBER ONE OR TWO!

[MUSIC NO. 4A "COCKTAIL MUSIC"]

(**DOROTHY** *goes to the Ladies Room.*)

JOHNNY. Is everything alright?

DAVID. Fine. Except that I've never been more uncomfortable in my whole life. How the hell did Dorothy find out about this party?

JOHNNY. We were talking on the phone this afternoon and I accidentally mentioned it. I'm sorry.

DAVID. You're sorry!

JOHNNY. Don't worry, Lorraine's a smart girl.

DAVID. Dorothy is smarter.

MICKEY. Hey… Johnny.

JOHNNY. *(To* **DAVID.***)* I'll see you later.

MICKEY. How long am I supposed to keep Rita company?

JOHNNY. Until she realizes that Edward is here.

EDWARD. *(To people at the bar.)* I was recently introduced to Mrs. Carnegie for the first time. And I said to her, jokingly of course, "It's fascinating to meet someone you always thought of as a hall." She wasn't amused either.

> *(***DOROTHY*** returning from the ladies' room approaches* **RITA.***)*

DOROTHY. Oh, you must be Rita. Johnny has spoken of you often. You know, it's very rare that my husband David and I weekend in the city. Generally we go to our place in Connecticut. It's removed but not remote, if you know what I mean. But a strange thing happened there recently. This woman… I don't know her name, of course… Moved into the neighborhood and rumor has it that she's psychic. I mean, she tells fortunes. Well, naturally everyone's very upset. God knows, we don't need another mystic in Connecticut.

> *("Cocktail Music" stops abruptly.)*

RITA. Have we met?

DOROTHY. *(Indignantly.)* Have we met?!!

> *(***DOROTHY*** goes back to her own table.)*

> *("Cocktail Music" resumes.)*

RITA. *(To* **MICKEY.***)* Come and sit down. You know something? I like you already.

MICKEY. Thanks, I like you too.

RITA. I want to know all about you.

MICKEY. Well, there's not much to tell.

RITA. Alright. Then we'll talk about me.

ROSIE. *(***GARY** *bringing a drink to* **ROSIE.***)* Oh... Gary, for me?

GARY. Yup.

ROSIE. Gary, I've missed you.

GARY. Hey the place hasn't been the same without you, Rosie. You know, Johnny hasn't let anyone sit on the piano since you left.

ROSIE. Oh?

GARY. Yeah. The place has changed. Johnny rarely does his act anymore. Tonight's the first night he's been dressed up in a long time.

ROSIE. Really?

GARY. Hey, I gotta get back to work. See you later.

ROSIE. Okay.

RITA. Have you worked here long?

MICKEY. Almost a year.

RITA. Do you like it?

MICKEY. Johnny's easy to work for.

RITA. Yes, he has a way with people doesn't he?

MICKEY. Mmmm...have you known him long?

RITA. Oh, yes.

MICKEY. I haven't seen you in here before.

RITA. No? Well...it has been a while. I travel a great deal. My work, you know...

MICKEY. What do you do?

RITA. I'm a stewardess. *(They laugh.)* No, I'm an actress.

MICKEY. Ah...have I seen you in anything?

RITA. Obviously not. Be a good boy and get Rita another drink.

MICKEY. Sure, Duchess.

RITA. Oh, I'm not a duchess.

MICKEY. I'm not a boy.

RITA. I could've been a duchess. I've played duchesses. I've played before duchesses.

MICKEY. But you're not a duchess.

> (*"Cocktail Music" fades.*)

> (**MICKEY** *goes to the bar to get* **RITA** *another drink.*)

RITA. No, I'm not. I was married to an earl once.
Excuse me. I thought you were still there.

MICKEY. (*To* **GARY**.) Give me another of whatever she's having.

GARY. Looks like you've got your hands full, Mickey.

MICKEY. I've had worse.

RITA. Actually I don't think he was an earl. I think his first name was Earl.

> (**RITA** *exits to the powder room.*)

[MUSIC NO. 5 "SHE TAKES VERY GOOD CARE OF HERSELF"]

GARY. You've had better.

MICKEY. Yeah, but I've had worse.

> SHE TAKES VERY GOOD CARE OF HERSELF,
> NEVER GOES OUT IN THE COLD.
> HER HAIR IS SOFT AND NICELY COIFFED
> BUT OH MY GOD IS SHE

GARY, PAUL & GEORGE.

> OLD?

GARY.

> SHE TAKES VERY GOOD CARE OF HERSELF,
> ROUGE ON HER PALLID CHEEK.

MICKEY.

> HER HAIR HAS SHEEN.

GARY.

> IT'S SQUEAKY CLEAN,

MICKEY & GARY.

> BUT OH MY GOD DOES SHE CREAK.

ALL FOUR.

> SHE SEARCHED FOR HER YOUTH
> BUT NEVER FOUND THE FOUNTAIN.

MICKEY.

SHE'S NOT OVER THE HILL, IN TRUTH.

ALL FOUR.

SHE'S OVER THE MOUNTAIN!

ALL.

SHE TAKES VERY GOOD CARE OF HERSELF,
CONSIDERS HER BEAUTY A GIFT.

PAUL & GEORGE.

SHE'S GOT NO BAGS, NOTHING SAGS.

MICKEY & GARY.

BUT OH MY GOD WHAT A LIFT CAN DO.

MICKEY, PAUL & GEORGE.

SHE SEARCHED FOR HER YOUTH.

GARY. *(Imitating an old woman.)* How I searched for it.

MICKEY, PAUL & GEORGE.

BUT NEVER FOUND THE FOUNTAIN.

GARY. Oh, let me tell ya boys…

ALL FOUR.

SHE'S NOT OVER THE HILL, IN TRUTH.
SHE'S OVER THE MOUNTAIN.

SHE TAKES VERY GOOD CARE OF HERSELF,
(A romantic sigh.) NEVER GOES OUT IN THE COLD.
HER HAIR IS SOFT. IT'S NICELY COIFFED.
HER HAIR HAS SHEEN. IT'S SQUEAKY CLEAN.
AHHH
BUT OH MY GOD IS SHE
OH MY GOD IS SHE
OH MY GOD IS SHE
OH MY GOD IS SHE

(**RITA** *re-enters.*)

(Whispered.) OLD!

(Lights down on the boys. Up on **RITA** *who has returned to her seat.* **JOHNNY** *has joined her.)*

[MUSIC NO. 5A "COCKTAIL MUSIC"]

JOHNNY. Rita, how do you do it? You never seem to age.

RITA. Well, you don't have to sound like you just found
Amelia Earhardt in the Men's Room. Oh, Johnny, I
want to thank you for the loan of Mickey. He's very
attractive.

JOHNNY. He's very expensive.

RITA. The best things are. I taught you that. But the
expensive ones are always the most trouble. They take
too much for granted.

JOHNNY. I see you're doing very well.

> *(He indicates a bracelet on her wrist.)*

RITA. A copy.

> *(He indicates a bracelet on the other wrist.)*

And these are copies of copies.

JOHNNY. Well, the chinchilla's not a copy.

RITA. Johnny, I've had this coat relined so many times
they're talking about zippers. Times are tough. They've
been tougher but that doesn't matter. *(To MICKEY.)*
I'd like to talk to Johnny alone. Why don't you do
something else now.

MICKEY. Like what?

RITA. Oh, I don't know. Why don't you go to the men's room
and say hello to Amelia.

MICKEY. Amelia who?

RITA. Oh, go away.

MICKEY. *(Leaving.)* Who's Amelia?

RITA. You see, what I mean, Johnny? Times are tough.
Service is slipping. I remember when people used to
do things right...with style! Where did all the good guys
go, Johnny? Where does everything go?

> *(Lights down on RITA and JOHNNY. Up on*
> *MICKEY and MAXIE at the bar.)*

MAXIE. Hey, Mickey. How ya doin' with the chinchilla?

MICKEY. She's okay. Sometimes I don't understand what
she's talking about.

MAXIE. Do you have to go to bed with her?

MICKEY. C'mon Maxie, she's a friend of Johnny's. Besides, I only have to stay with her till she realizes that whats-his-name is here. They're old friends. Johnny's playing one of his little games.

MAXIE. Well, would you have gone to bed with her? For a price, I mean. Hey, I'm sorry. None of my business. I just haven't been able to figure you out. You seem like a bright guy. Haven't you ever thought of doing anything else with your life?

MICKEY. Look. I like parties. I like to drink. I like expensive clothes. And I don't know how to do anything else.

(Lights back up on **JOHNNY** *and* **RITA.***)*

RITA. But you still haven't told me what the occasion is.

JOHNNY. You're here.

RITA. That's very sweet, Johnny, but I don't believe you. I think I'd like my escort back now if you don't mind.

JOHNNY. He's coming.

(He beckons for **EDWARD** *who sits down with* **RITA.***)*

RITA. Aren't you at the wrong table?

EDWARD. I came to say hello, Rita.

("Cocktail Music" fades out.)

RITA. Oh, I get it. You're an old fan of mine. An autograph. Is that what you want, dear?

EDWARD. You were very beautiful.

RITA. Yes I was. Why is everybody talking about me in the past tense tonight? What is this? A surprise wake?

EDWARD. I was about to say you haven't changed. I loved you very much.

RITA. Edward. EDWARD! What are you doing here?

EDWARD. Something about a puzzle.

RITA. Johnny's idea.

EDWARD. We're all Johnny's idea tonight. He's turning on us for all the bad advice we gave him.

RITA. Well, he has that right. Where have you been all these years?

EDWARD. I could ask you the same question. I lost track of you. God, I haven't seen you since...

RITA. Quiet! There are children in the room.

EDWARD. But I've kept up with Johnny.

RITA. Me too. *(Pause.)* Are you still waiting for your ship to come in?

EDWARD. It came in. Don't you remember? There was a dock strike.

What about you, Rita?

RITA. Oh me, well, I guess I've been married since I saw you.

EDWARD. Oh, I've heard. Several times.

RITA. Oh...

EDWARD. How many is that?

RITA. That's like counting drinks. What's the point? But I am between engagements. That's very cute, isn't it?

EDWARD. I was third, wasn't I?

RITA. Third what?

EDWARD. Husband.

RITA. Second.

EDWARD. Third. I'm sure.

RITA. No. I'm sure you were the second because...

EDWARD. You're mind is slipping.

RITA. My mind is not. Oh...perhaps you were the third.

EDWARD. No, I was the second.

RITA. Oh, damn you. That's precisely why you were not the last. There's nothing more ridiculous than an aging brat.

EDWARD. To old times.

RITA. To old times. *(Glasses clink.)*

EDWARD. I can still see you sitting on a steamer trunk. The upper deck. That luxury liner.

RITA. The Titanic!

EDWARD. I never needed reservations.

RITA. I always *had* reservations.

EDWARD. Those south of France summers. That season in Georgia trying out the show. We were someone's guest.

RITA. We were always someone's guest. Remember, it was an honest-to-God knock-your-eyes-out plantation.

EDWARD. Complete with veranda.

RITA. And servants. My special occasion tiara.

EDWARD. There were lots of special occasions.

RITA. The diamond brooch.

EDWARD. It took two months of royalty checks to pay for it.

RITA. I thought you paid for the sapphire lavalier.

EDWARD. No. I always wondered who gave you that.

RITA. What difference does it make? It was only money.

EDWARD. It was always money.

RITA. And winters in New York.

[MUSIC NO. 6 "LUXURY"]

It used to snow. Cab drivers spoke English. And my chinchilla was just a baby then.

WHERE IS MY TIARA?
WHERE'S MY LAVALIER?
WHERE'S MY DIAMOND BROOCH?
HAVE YOU SEEN IT, MY DEAR?

EDWARD.

WHERE IS MY LIBRETTO?
WHERE'S MY PAD AND PEN?
WHERE IS MY MANUSCRIPT?
HAVE YOU SEEN IT, MY FRIEND?

BOTH.

WHERE'S THE SWING ON THE VERANDA
WHERE WE FIRST MET?
AND WHERE IS THE VERANDA?
HOW COULD WE FORGET?

EDWARD.

> WHERE DOES THE TIME GO?
> HOW DOES THE TIME FLY?
> ISN'T IT TIME I
> HAD A FEW ANSWERS?

RITA.

> WHERE DOES THE TIME GO?
> HOW DOES THE TIME FLY?
> ISN'T IT TIME I
> HAD A FEW ANSWERS?
>
> VILLAS IN THE SOUTH OF FRANCE,

EDWARD.

> HIDEAWAYS IN ROME.

BOTH.

> TOWNHOUSES IN LONDON,
> BUT I HAVE HAD NO HOME.

EDWARD.

> LIVING ON THE COTE D'AZUR
> IN THE BEST OF TASTE.

RITA.

> IN THE LAP OF LUXURY.

BOTH.

> LIVING IN HASTE... WHAT A WASTE!
>
> PROPERTY ON THE MEDITERRANEAN,
> GRAND CORNICHE ABOVE.
> SUNBURNT LOVERS BY THE BARREL.
> PRECIOUS LITTLE LOVE.

RITA.

> WHERE IS MY TIARA?
> WHERE'S MY LAVALIER?
> WHERE'S MY DIAMOND BROOCH?

EDWARD.

> I STILL SEE IT, MY DEAR.
> WHERE IS MY LIBRETTO?
> WHERE'S MY PAD AND PEN?
> WHERE IS MY MANUSCRIPT?

RITA.

> I STILL SEE IT, MY FRIEND.

> LOOK, THE POT OF GOLD.
> LOOK, THE UPPER DECKS.

EDWARD.

> LOOK FOR LOVE.

BOTH.

> SETTLE FOR LESS.

> WHERE DOES THE TIME GO?
> HOW DOES THE TIME FLY?
> ISN'T IT TIME I
> HAD A FEW ANSWERS?
> WHERE DOES THE TIME GO?
> HOW DOES THE TIME FLY?
> WHERE DOES THE TIME GO?

[MUSIC NO. 6A "COCKTAIL MUSIC"]

MICKEY. *(To* **JOHNNY.***)* It worked. You sure know people. I'll offer this as a parting gesture.

> *(***MICKEY** *approaches* **RITA***'s table with a bottle of wine.)* More wine?

RITA. Ah. There you are. You shouldn't leave me alone for so long. Edward, I'd like you to meet my friend. What is your name?

MICKEY. Mickey.

RITA. Mickey. As a matter of fact you're sitting in his seat.

EDWARD. I was just leaving. Come, sit down. You haven't changed, Rita. Too bad.

> *(***EDWARD** *goes over to* **JOHNNY.***)*

RITA. *(To* **MICKEY.***)* That man is totally senile. He's old enough to be my... Pour!

> *(Lights down on* **MICKEY** *and* **RITA.** *Up on* **JOHNNY** *and* **EDWARD.***)*

EDWARD. I thought she was delighted to see me. But I guess not. Would you mind if I left?

JOHNNY. Yes, I'd mind. I want you to be here.

EDWARD. Alright. I'll be at the bar. Are these girls available? For conversation?

JOHNNY. Sure. Maxie, talk to this guy.

MAXIE. Hello, again.

EDWARD. Can I get you a drink?

MAXIE. Oh please. Let me get you one. It's for the cause.

EDWARD. The cause?

MAXIE. Equality.

EDWARD. What a curious idea. Excuse me.

(**EDWARD** *goes to the bar.*)

GARY. Hey Maxie, Nice party, huh?

MAXIE. I've seen better. This place is really starting to get me down. I haven't been picked up in weeks.

GARY. It's the wrong kind of place.

MAXIE. You're tellin' me. This place is so square it gives me a headache. All I ever meet are married men and I haven't had to stoop to that.

FRANCINE. C'mon, Lorraine. Let's change.

MAXIE. *(To* **GARY.***)* Why does she get all the breaks?

GARY. She knows how to stoop.

MAXIE. All I get is that old New York routine. "I'd invite you up for drink, but I don't drink."

GARY. Or "I'm having my period."

MAXIE. That one I've never heard. Thank, God.

GARY. If things get really tough, you could probably rent Mickey for the night.

MAXIE. I'm not renting anything. Besides, I'm not too sure about him. I think he swings both ways. Now, Johnny. That's another story. If he ever decides to change his mind...

GARY. You know I think he's still stuck on Rosie. But cheer up, Maxie. Something'll turn up.

MAXIE. Gary, you knock me out. Nothing bothers you. You're so cool all the time. How do you do it?

GARY. I'm totally high.

ROSIE. *(To* **JOHNNY.***)* You have a nice crop of girls this year. Are they all in love with you?

JOHNNY. No.

ROSIE. The blonde one's a knockout.

JOHNNY. Lorraine? Unfortunately David thinks so too.

ROSIE. Are you deliberately trying to start trouble?

("Cocktail Music" fades out.)

JOHNNY. No. I don't want any trouble. You know what I want? I want you to sing me a song.

ROSIE. Is that why you invited me here? I don't hear from you for a year and you want me to sing?

JOHNNY. That's not fair.

ROSIE. You walked out on me, Johnny. I don't have to be fair.

[MUSIC NO. 7 "I'LL SING YOUR FAVORITE SONG"]

SAME OLD JOHNNY.
SAME OLD PIANO.
SAME OLD SAD REFRAIN
SAME OLD CROWD SINGING THE SAME OLD SONG,
STANDIN' IN THE SAME OLD RAIN.

*(**ROSIE** sings the song straight out to the audience.)*

YOU MAY THINK THAT SITTING ON A PIANO
REQUIRES NO SPECIAL KNACK.
BUT IT'S HARD ON THE LEGS,
HELL ON THE STOCKINGS, AND OH, MY ACHING BACK.
BUT...
I'LL SING YOUR FAVORITE SONG
THOUGH THE WORDS AREN'T RIGHT
AND IT FEELS ALL WRONG.
THE WORLD'S BEEN CRUEL
BUT WHO'S TO BLAME IT?
YOU GOT A FAV'RITE SONG?
WELL, BUSTER, STEP RIGHT UP AND NAME IT AND

ROSIE.

> I'LL SING YOUR FAVORITE TUNE.
> BUY ME A DRINK AND I'LL JUNE, MOON, SPOON.
> YOU'LL GO OUT BELIEVING
> IT'S BEEN A FINE DAY
> COURTESY OF ME, MYSELF
> AND MY MISTER STEINWAY.
>
> "OVER THE RAINBOW?" ANYTIME.
> I GOT A REAL SAD ARRANGEMENT OF "FUNNY
>   VALENTINE."
> YOU WANT "FASCINATIN' RHYTHM?"
> SURE, WHY NOT!
> "HERE'S THAT RAINY DAY AGAIN"
> NOW THERE'S A HOT NUMBER.
> I'LL EVEN SING "SWANEE" IF YOU'LL LOWER THE KEY,
> LOWER THE KEY... LOWER THE...
> THANK YOU KINDLY, MISTER PIANO MAN.
>
> I'LL SING YOUR FAVORITE SONG.
> I'LL CROON IT LOW.
> I'LL BELT IT STRONG.
> I'LL SING THE BLUES.
> I DON'T MEAN MAYBE.
> ISN'T ANYBODY OUT THERE
> GONNA ASK FOR "MELANCHOLY BABY?"
>
> COME TO ME AND I'LL SING YOUR FAVORITE SONG
> THOUGH THE WORDS AREN'T RIGHT
> AND IT FEELS ALL WRONG.
> THE WORLD'S BEEN CRUEL
> BUT WHO CAN BLAME IT?
> YOU GOT A FAV'RITE SONG?
> WELL, BUSTER, STEP RIGHT UP AND, STEP RIGHT UP AND
> STEP RIGHT UP AND NAME IT
>
> AND I'LL SING YOUR FAVORITE TUNE.
> BUY ME A DRINK AND I'LL JUNE, MOON, SPOON.
> YOU'LL GO OUT BELIEVING
> IT'S BEEN A FINE DAY.

AND I GUARANTEE I'LL MAKE YOU BELIEVE,
OH, I'LL MAKE YOU BELIEVE,
OH, I KNOW YOU'LL BELIEVE EV'RY WORD I SAY.

> *(Lights down on* **ROSIE** *and up on* **DAVID** *and* **DOROTHY**.*)*

DOROTHY. Did you ever expect Johnny to be so successful with the club?

DAVID. Yes, I did. But I'm worried about him. He's not the same. Even the way he dresses. He's not the playboy anymore. You grow up, and that's a shame. I miss the flamboyance.

DOROTHY. Vicarious friends are the most satisfying aren't they, dear. Imagine if you had to do your own living.

DAVID. You are such a pain in the ass.

DOROTHY. You...

[MUSIC NO. 8 "JOHNNY'S GIRLS / A CONTINENTAL GUY"]

> *(Lights up on the Club Stage.)*

GARY. Ladies and gentlemen, say "Hello" to Johnny's Girls!

MAXIE, GLORIA, LORRAINE & FRANCINE.

THANK YOU FOR THE CANDY, MISTER.
THANK YOU FOR THE FLOWERS.
THANK YOU FOR THE BRAND NEW DRESS.
WE'RE THE LADIES OF THE CHORUS.
WE KNOW THAT YOU ADORE US.
BUT FRANKLY, WE COULDN'T CARE LESS!
SO YOU CAN KEEP YOUR FLOWERS
SAVE YOUR COMPLIMENTS.
WE'LL TAKE WHAT THE MANAGEMENT
PROUDLY PRESENTS.

> *(**JOHNNY** appears. He is Mr. Suave, Playboy of the world. Accompanied by* **LORRAINE**, **GLORIA**, **FRANCINE** *and* **MAXIE**.*)*

JOHNNY.

I'M A BLACK TIE, AN OLD SILK HAT,
A CONTINENTAL GUY, A SPOTLESS SPAT.
I'M HAPPY DAYS NEVER UNDER THE WEATHER.
MY DANCING SHOES ARE MADE OF PATENT LEATHER.

I'M SOPHISTICATION, EVERY PARTY'S HIT.
GOT A REPUTATION THAT JUST WON'T QUIT.
BIG BLACK CAR, SETTING TRENDS.
HEDY LAMARR, WE'RE JUST GOOD FRIENDS.

OH THERE AIN'T NO LIFE LIKE THE LIFE IN THE MOVIES.
THERE AIN'T NO LIFE, LIKE THE LIFE ON THE SCREEN.
THERE AIN'T NO LIFE LIKE THE LIFE IN THE MOVIES,
OH THERE AIN'T NO LIFE LIKE THE LIFE ON THE SCREEN.

JOHNNY.

I SPENT A FORTUNE KEEPING EV'RY HAIR IN PLACE.
GOT A MILLION DOLLAR SMILE CAPPED ON MY FACE.
LOOKING LIKE AN AD FOR MARTINI AND ROSSI,
I'M AN EIGHT BY TEN INCH GLOSSY.

JOHNNY.	**GIRLS.**
I'M SOPHISTICATION, MISTER CHIC.	JOHNNY
INVITATIONS EVERY DAY OF THE WEEK.	JOHNNY
BOBO ROCKEFELLER CALLS ME "DARLING".	OOH

JOHNNY.

BARBARA HUTTON CALLS ME "DEAR".
AND EV'RYBODY HOLDS ME IN THE HIGHEST ESTEEM
BUT NOBODY HOLDS ME NEAR ON A COLD AND
DREARY WINTER'S EV'NING.
NOBODY HOLDS ME NEAR.

THE GIRLS.

I'LL HOLD YOU NEAR.

JOHNNY.

NOBODY HOLDS ME NEAR.

THE GIRLS.

I'LL HOLD YOU NEAR.

JOHNNY.

NOBODY HOLDS ME...

GIRLS.

THERE AIN'T NO LIFE LIKE... LIFE IN THE MOVIES.
THERE AIN'T NO LIFE LIKE... LIFE IN THE MOVIES.

JOHNNY.

IF THERE AIN'T NO LIFE LIKE THE LIFE IN THE MOVIES

JOHNNY.	**GIRLS.**
THERE AIN'T NO LIFE AT ALL.	DOOT, DOOT, DOOT, DOOT, DOOT, DOOT, DOOT

JOHNNY & GIRLS.

IF THERE AIN'T NO LIFE LIKE THE LIFE IN THE MOVIES
THERE AIN'T NO LIFE AT ALL.

JOHNNY.

I'M A BLACK TIE.

GIRLS.

MY, OH, MY!

JOHNNY.

I'M A CONTINENTAL...

GIRLS.

HE'S A CONTINENTAL...

JOHNNY.

I'M A CONTNIENTAL GUY!

[MUSIC NO. 8A "PLAYOFF - COCKTAIL MUSIC"]

(Lights down on the club stage. Up on **RITA** *and* **MICKEY.***)*

RITA. Now that's the old Johnny. Ah, Hollywood. Johnny visited me once.

MICKEY. Were you in the movies?

RITA. A few. I didn't make a go of it though. They said I was too big to be captured on celluloid.

EDWARD. *(From across the room.)* HAH!

RITA. In stature! They were talking about stature. *(To* **MICKEY.***)* When I left Hollywood, it was Katharine

Hepburn's lucky day. She got all my parts. Ah, Hollywood. It's not there anymore. Things change.

MICKEY. Not fast enough.

RITA. Oh, you wait. Younger men get older...fast. Fortunately older women don't.

MICKEY. How convenient.

RITA. Hell, I started getting older the day I was born. I started measuring things by the end of them, asking myself how much time is left.

MICKEY. Not much.

RITA. You have no feelings.

MICKEY. But I'm good looking.

RITA. Not for long. Those little lines around the eyes... already! Telling us tales we've all been bored by a thousand times. And then what? The party ends. The band goes home. And your face falls off. Take it from me, kiddo. The future is in plastic surgery.

> (*"Cocktail Music" fades out.*)

> (**GARY** *sniffs some cocaine as* **JOHNNY** *walks in.*)

JOHNNY. Hey Gary, take it easy on that stuff. You're gonna burn your brains out.

GARY. What brains?

MAXIE. Johnny, you got a minute?

JOHNNY. Sure, Maxie.

MAXIE. I been working up this new number with the band and...

JOHNNY. Maxie. I told you when I hired you I didn't need another featured singer.

MAXIE. Sorry I even mentioned it.

> (**LORRAINE** *enters.*)

> (*"Cocktail Music 8a" resumes.*)

JOHNNY. New costume?

LORRAINE. I've been saving it.

JOHNNY. Let me give you some advice, Lorraine. If you're trying to break up a marriage it's best to wait till after the holidays.

LORRAINE. That's provided you can get through the holidays. Why'd he have to bring her here, Johnny?

JOHNNY. I invited both of them.

LORRAINE. You what?

JOHNNY. I thought if you saw them together you'd realize how impossible your situation is. I'm sorry.

LORRAINE. I don't blame you. Married men. It's not the first time it's happened to me.

JOHNNY. I know. And David has been sneaking in here for years.

LORRAINE. But it's different this time. I think I have a chance with David.

JOHNNY. I think... I think it's hard to forget people.

LORRAINE. Are you still in love with her?

JOHNNY. Rosie? No. Oh, I don't know. I was never very good at love. It slowed me down too much.

LORRAINE. What's happening tonight?

JOHNNY. Not now. Not yet.

("Cocktail Music" out.)

MAXIE. Lorraine. It's time for your number.

LORRAINE. Maxie, go away!

MAXIE. Look, Lorraine. Work it out on your own time.

LORRAINE. Maxie!

MAXIE. Alright. I know the number.

LORRAINE. Maxie, don't take another step. See ya later Johnny.

MAXIE. Break a leg, honey. Both of them.

[MUSIC NO. 9 "MORNING MAN"]

LORRAINE.

A MAN GETS WHAT HE WANTS
AND THEN HE'S UP AND THEN HE'S OUT.
HE'S OUT THE DOOR BEFORE YOU'VE EVEN HAD A
    WARNING.
OH, IT'S EASY ALL RIGHT
TO GET A MAN FOR THE NIGHT,
BUT WHERE IS MY MAN FOR THE MORNING?

SOMEBODY ELSE'S HUSBAND IS AN EASY MARK FOR
    SUPPER.
IT'S LIKE PICKING RIPE BANANAS OFF A BUNCH.
ASK ANY BEGINNER, IT'S EASY TO GET A MAN FOR DINNER
BUT WHERE IS MY MAN FOR BRUNCH?
MORNING MAN... MORNING MAN... MORNING MAN...

GLORIA.

OOH, BACON'S ON THE TABLE

LORRAINE.

MORNING MAN...

GLORIA.

OOH, EGGS ARE GONNA FRY.

LORRAINE.

MORNING MAN...

GLORIA.	**FRANCINE.**
OOH, MILK IS IN THE CREAMER.	THE COFFEE'S PERCOLATIN' DON'T KEEP HIM WAITIN'.

LORRAINE.

MORNING MAN...

GLORIA.	**FRANCINE.**
OOH, SUGAR'S IN THE BOWL.	POUR IT PIPIN' HOT IN HIS FAVORITE CUP.

LORRAINE.	**GLORIA & FRANCINE.**
MORNING MAN...	OOH...

ALL.

ONCE OVER EASY ON THE EGSS OR SUNNYSIDE UP?

LORRAINE, FRANCINE & GLORIA.

A MAN GETS WHAT HE WANTS,

AND THEN HE'S UP THEN HE'S OUT.

HE'S OUT THE DOOR WITHOUT A WARNING.

IT'S EASY ALRIGHT

TO GET A MAN FOR THE NIGHT

LORRAINE.

BUT

LORRAINE, FRANCINE & GLORIA.

WHERE IS MY MAN...

I NEED MY MORNING MAN...

GLORIA & FRANCINE.

OOH, BACON'S ON THE TABLE...

LORRAINE.

MORNIN' MAN

GLORIA & FRANCINE.

OOH EGGS ARE GONNA FRY...

LORRAINE.

MORNIN' MAN...

GLORIA.

OOH, MILK IS IN THE
CREAMER...

FRANCINE.

YOU KNOW THERE'S
NEVER BEEN
A QUEEN OF FARINA

LORRAINE.

MORNIN' MAN...

GLORIA.

OOH, SUGAR'S IN THE
BOWL

FRANCINE.

LIKE THE ONE YOU GOT.

SHE SERVES IT PIPING
HOT.

LORRAINE.

MORNIN' MAN

GLORIA.

> MORNIN' MAN

FRANCINE.

> MORNIN' MAN

LORRAINE.

> MORNIN' MAN

GLORIA.

> MORNIN' MAN

FRANCINE.

> MORNIN' MAN

LORRAINE.

> MORNIN' MAN

GLORIA & FRANCINE.

> MORNIN' MAN, OOH

LORRAINE.

> YOU'RE THE ONLY ONE CAN SAVE ME...
> MORNIN' MAN.

> > *(Lights fade on* **LORRAINE.** *Up on* **DAVID** *and* **DOROTHY.***)*

DOROTHY. She's doing that deliberately.

DAVID. What?

DOROTHY. That girl. She was singing that to you.

DAVID. You're hallucinating.

DOROTHY. You're infuriating.

DAVID. I'd rather be hallucinating.

DOROTHY. I have a headache.

DAVID. You are a headache.

DOROTHY. I want a divorce.

DAVID. Bartender, the lady would like a divorce.

GARY. Straight up?

DOROTHY. On the rocks!

RITA. Do you like the term "gigolo"?

MICKEY. No.

RITA. You prefer escort?

MICKEY. That's better.

RITA. Do you escort often?

MICKEY. Sometimes.

RITA. I guess that's how you became such an exciting conversationalist.

GARY. Lorraine. Your number was terrific.

MAXIE. Yeah. That was really swell, Lorraine.

LORRAINE. Thanks.

MAXIE. Just one little thing bothered me.

LORRAINE. Oh?

MAXIE. I think one of your falsies is slipping.

LORRAINE. Maxie, do me a favor. Ask Gary to make you a screwdriver. And sit on it!

DOROTHY. She's so vulgar.

DAVID. Dorothy, you've had enough to drink.

DOROTHY. Enough? They don't *have* enough!

[MUSIC NO. 10 "REMARKABLE"]

Do you know why I drink, David? Because after I arrange the flowers, after I give instructions to the help, and after I explain once more to your sons why you missed dinner the night before, and after I have that last lonely cup of morning coffee, I have nothing else to do!!

LORRAINE. Why are they still together?

GLORIA. Forget him, honey.

MAXIE. Cheer up, Lorraine. I hear they're building a home for wayward chorus girls.

FRANCINE. Maxie, leave her alone. Now, I mean it!

MAXIE. Shut up.

GLORIA. You shut up.

MAXIE. Don't tell me to shut up.

(*Fight escalates.*)

GARY. Girls! Girls! Stop it!

EDWARD. Maybe I should leave.

FRANCINE. Oh, sit down! This party's just getting started.

DOROTHY. Now I can see why you never brought me here. It's a long way from Sutton Place.

DAVID. Dorothy, don't drink anymore.

DOROTHY. Don't tell me what to do.

DAVID. Keep your voice down. Do you want to make a fool of yourself?

DOROTHY. No. But I wouldn't mind making a fool out of you.

DAVID.

YOU'RE A REMARKABLE WOMAN.

DOROTHY.

YOU'RE A REMARKABLE MAN.

BOTH.

WATCH OUR DUST. WATCH OUR SPARKS.
WE'RE SO REMARKABLE THEY'RE MAKING REMARKS
ABOUT WHAT A REMARKABLE COMBINATION.
WHAT A REMARKABLE PAIR.

DAVID.

YOU'RE GETTING ON MY NERVES

DOROTHY.

YOU'RE GETTING INTO MY HAIR

RITA.

WHAT A REMARKABLE ESCORT

DAVID.

YOU'RE A REMARKABLE WOMAN

MICKEY.

WHAT AN APPRECIATIVE DATE

DOROTHY.

YOU'RE A REMARKABLE MAN

RITA.

WATCH YOUR FANGS

MICKEY.
WATCH YOUR CLAWS

DAVID & DOROTHY.
WATCH OUR DUST
WATCH OUR SPARKS

RITA & MICKEY.
WE'RE SO REMARKABLE
THERE
OUGHTTA BE LAWS
AGAINST
SUCH AN UNBEATABLE
COMBINATION
SUCH A REMARKABLE
TEAM

WE'RE SO REMARKABLE

WHAT A REMARKABLE
COMBINATION
WHAT A REMARKABLE
TEAM

MICKEY.
MEET MISS AMERICA

DAVID.
YOU'RE GETTING ON MY
NERVES

RITA.
MEET MISTER AMERICAN
DREAM

DOROTHY.
YOU'RE GETTING INTO MY
HAIR

LORRAINE.
DID YOU

DOROTHY.
WHAT A REMARK-
ABLE
COMBINATION

WHAT A REMARK-
ABLE

TEAM

DAVID.
SUCH A
REMARK-
ABLE
TEAM

MICKEY.
MEET MISS

LORRAINE.
SEE THE

WAY SHE

TREATS HIM?

GET A
DIVORCE

DAVID.

YOU'RE GETTING ON MY NERVES	AMERICA	GET A DIVORCE

DOROTHY.   **RITA.**

YOU'RE GETTING INTO MY HAIR	MEET MR. AMERICAN DREAM	DAVID, GET A DIVORCE

MAXIE.

SHE'S SUCH A TERRIBLE DANCER

DAVID.   **RITA.**

YOU'RE A REMARKABLE WOMAN	WHAT A REMARKABLE ESCORT

MAXIE.

WHAT'S MORE, HIS SINGING IS FLAT

DOROTHY.   **MICKEY.**

YOU'RE A REMARKABLE MAN	WHAT AN APPRECIATIVE DATE

MAXIE.   **DAVID & DOROTHY.**   **RITA.**

JESUS CHRIST, FOR MAXIE'S SAKE	WATCH OUR DUST	WATCH YOUR FANGS

                                        MICKEY.

MISER PRODUCER WON'T YOU GIVE ME A BREAK	WATCH OUR SPARKS WE'RE SO REMARK- ABLE	WATCH YOUR CLAWS WE'RE SO REMARK- ABLE

MAXIE.	DOROTHY, DAVID & RITA	LORRAINE.	FRANCINE.	GLORIA.
PLEASE GET ME OUT		DID YOU	GIMME, GIMME	BITCH
OF THE CHORUS		SEE THE	GIMME, GIMME	BITCH
	WHAT A		GIMME, GIMME	BITCH
GIVE ME THE	REMARK-ABLE / UNBEAT-ABLE	WAY SHE	ME	BITCH
CHANCE I	COMBINA-TION		GIMME, GIMME	BITCH
			GIMME, GIMME	BITCH
DESERVE	WHAT A REMARK-ABLE	TREATS HIM	GIMME, GIMME	BITCH
	PAIR/DREAM		ME	BITCH
	DAVID.		ISN'T SHE A	
QUICK BEFORE I GO	YOU'RE GETTING ON MY	GET A DIVORCE	TROUBLE MAKER	BITCH, BITCH
TO POT	NERVES	GET A DIVORCE		BITCH, BITCH
MAXIE.	**DOROTHY.**	**LORRAINE.**	**FRANCINE.**	**GLORIA.**
BEFORE I RUN OUT OF	YOU'RE GET-TING INTO MY	DAVE, GET A DIVORCE	ONE MORE WORD	BITCH, BITCH
			AND I WILL BLOW MY	BITCH, BITCH
NERVE	HAIR		TOP.	BITCH

JOHNNY. *Stop it!!* Will everyone, please sit down.

RITA. This is a terrible party.

(Lots of chatter.)

JOHNNY. Everybody, I have an announcement. I'm selling the club. I'm leaving New York...for good.

(A beat of stunned silence.)

GARY. Hey, hey, nobody leaves New York for good.

DAVID. Where the hell are you going?

MAXIE. You can't go, Johnny. You just can't.

JOHNNY. Take it easy, Maxie. There are other jobs.

MAXIE. Sure. Back on the road. I can't do it. I'll die out there.

JOHNNY. You won't die.

MAXIE. That's even worse.

DOROTHY. I think we should leave.

DAVID. Sit down.

DOROTHY. I have a headache.

LORRAINE. Oh, shut up.

JOHNNY. Please, everybody. I've been thinking about this for a long time. But I've got to clear the air before I go.

RITA. Then get a ventilator.

JOHNNY. Rita, you could help me now. You know things.

RITA. I don't know anything.

JOHNNY. Nothing?

RITA. Nothing!

JOHNNY. That's what it comes to, doesn't it? Nothing. Every time I turn the lights out here and go home, I go home to nothing. Well, I need *something*.

[MUSIC NO. 11 "NEW YORK IS DRIVING ME CRAZY"]

ROSIE. You need something? You're kicking everybody out in the street and you want a sendoff. Is that it? Well, somebody make a note to have a band at the station.

JOHNNY.

NEW YORK IS DRIVING ME CRAZY.
THIS CLUB IS DRIVING ME NUTS!

I WOULD'VE LEFT SOONER,
BUT BOY, I'VE BEEN LAZY
AND I NEVER HAD THE GUTS BEFORE
BUT NOW I DO, I'M GONNA GO, I'M GONNA GET...

Out of this town. New York is pulling me down the drain and I'm not going! I'm getting out!

OUTTA THIS TOWN WITH ITS SCREECHING TAXIS,
FAR AWAY FOR MY OWN SWEET SAKE.
OUTTA THIS TOWN WITH ITS SAD LITTLE MAXIES
AND ROSIES WHO CAN'T GET A BREAK.
AWAY FROM THE PARTY, THE PIPER TO PAY
AND RITA WHO'S STILL GOT NOTHING TO SAY.
OUTTA THE GRASP AND OUTTA THE CLUTCH
OF PLATINUM BLONDES WHO ASK TOO MUCH.

THE STREETS ARE CRAWLING WITH HIGH CLASS WHORES.
THEY WEAR CHANELS. THEY WEAR DIORS.
YOU SEE THE SIGNS. YOU SEE THE SCENES
OF BURNED OUT BOYS AND FLAMING QUEENS.
CHORUS GIRLS GET BURIED ALIVE,
SING FOR THEIR SUPPER IN A SMOKEY DIVE.
THEY LOOK FOR LOVE AND SETTLE FOR SEX
AND SELL THEIR SOULS FOR SIZABLE CHECKS.
GIVE ME ONE GOOD REASON WHY
YOU THINK THAT I SHOULD SACRIFICE MY LIFE
AND STICK AROUND.

JOHNNY.	ROSIE.	ALL.
I	THINK OF THE TIMES WE HAD TOGETHER	
DON'T		THINK OF THE CLUB, YOU CAN'T GO FREE
CARE	"BLUE SKIES", "STORMY WEATHER"	

NOW, DON'T STOP ME!		IF NOT FOR YOU THEN WHAT ABOUT ME	IF NOT FOR YOU THEN WHAT ABOUT ME
JOHNNY.	**ROSIE.**	**GIRLS.**	**GUYS.**
I		WHAT A GOOD TIME TO PULL THE RUG OUT	WHAT A REMARK-ABLE
NEED	WHAT A REMARK-ABLE	WHAT A GOOD TIME TO HAVE A FIT	SITUATION
AIR.	SITUATION	WHAT A GOOD TIME TO LOSE YOUR SENSES	WHAT A REMARK-ABLE
PLEASE, DON'T STOP ME!	WHAT A TIME TO QUIT.	WHAT A GOOD TIME TO QUIT.	TIME TO QUIT.

JOHNNY.

ONE MORE NIGHT HERE
I CAN'T TAKE IT
GIMME ONE MORE DRINK OR
I WON'T MAKE IT

GUYS.

STICK AROUND OR WE WONT MAKE IT

JOHNNY & GUYS.	**GIRLS.**
THROUGH	WHAT A REMARKABLE
TO –	SUCH A REMARKABLE
NIGHT	NIGHT

ACT TWO

[MUSIC NO. 11A "NEW YORK IS DRIVING ME CRAZY – REPRISE"]

JOHHNY.

> ONE MORE NIGHT HERE
> I CAN'T TAKE IT
> GIMME ONE MORE DRINK OR
> I WONT MAKE IT

GUYS.

> STICK AROUND OR WE WON'T MAKE IT

JOHNNY & GUYS.	**GIRLS.**
THROUGH	WHAT A REMARKABLE
TO –	SUCH A REMARKABLE
NIGHT	NIGHT

GARY. You can't leave, Johnny.

GLORIA. Johnny, listen to him.

RITA. Johnny, I don't want to hear about unfinished business. You can't wrap your life up in a neat little package and drop it in the garbage on the way to the airport.

ROSIE. You mean to tell me, you invited me here to say goodbye? We did that already. You can't keep saying goodbye. You lose credibility.

LORRAINE. I'm getting out of here before I scratch somebody's eyes out.

> (**LORRAINE** *exits to the dressing room.*)

MICKEY. Johnny, I'm not ready to go back on the streets.

GARY. You run the best club in New York.

MICKEY. The service is great.

GARY. The clientele is terrific.

GLORIA. And the atmosphere is always so…

FRANCINE. Festive.

MAXIE. And the ladies room is always spotless. Well, that's important.

[MUSIC NO. 12 "WHERE IN THE WORLD IS THE WORLD I WANTED"]

(*JOHNNY is in a single spotlight as he reveals more of his thoughts. The others don't hear this.*)

JOHNNY.

IS ANYBODY LIST'NING?
IS ANYBODY THERE?
I TALK ABOUT MY TROUBLES
BUT NO ONE SEEMS TO CARE.
I DON'T KNOW WHAT I WANT.
MY FUTURE ISN'T CLEAR.
THE ONLY THING I KNOW IS
I KNOW IT ISN'T HERE.

WHERE IN THE WORLD IS THE WORLD THAT I WANTED?
WHO IN THE WORLD UNDERSTANDS?
HOW IN THE WORLD DID THE GIRL THAT I WANTED
MANAGE TO SLIP THROUGH MY HANDS?

LIKE SANDS FROM THE SEASHORE
ESCAPING MY FINGERS.
THE DREAM FLIES AWAY
BUT THE MEMORY LINGERS.
I HAD A CERTAIN FLAIR, A CONTINENTAL AIR,
ALWAYS MISTER TRÈS DEBONAIRE.

I WAS A MAN WITH A DREAM TO SPARE.
A MAN WITH A DREAM TO SHARE.
MUST I BE A MAN WHO'S TRAPPED
TRYING TO ADAPT
TO AN OVERWHELMING FEELING OF DESPAIR?
HOW IN THE WORLD DID THE SINGING AND THE
    DANCING
GET SO FAR AWAY FROM MY HEART?

I FORGOT ALL THE QUESTIONS
AND QUESTIONED THE ANSWERS.
I'VE GOT TO MAKE A NEW START.

WANTING TO BREAK LOOSE
AND GO WHERE THE WIND BLOWS.
UP THROUGH THE CHIMNEY
AND OUT THROUGH THE WINDOWS.
AWAY FROM THIS TOWN
BEFORE I BREAK DOWN
I'M FEELING LIKE A MAN WHO'S DROWNING.

I WAS A MAN WITH A DREAM TO SPARE,
A MAN WITH A DREAM TO SHARE.
MUST I BE A MAN WHO'S LOST,
MY STARS FOREVER CROSSED
BY THAT OVERWHELMING QUESTION...

WHERE IN THE WORLD IS THE WORLD THAT I WANTED?
WHERE IN THE WORLD IS THE GIRL?
WHERE IS THE LIFE, THE WIFE THAT I WANTED?
WHERE IN THE WORLD IS THE WORLD?
WHERE IN THE, WHERE IN THE, WHERE IN THE WORLD?
DOES ANYBODY KNOW?
BUT TOMORROW, TOMORROW, TOMORROW WILL BE
     DIFF'RENT.
THE ANSWER TO THE QUESTION IS... "GO".

(Lights restore as action continues.)

EDWARD. Johnny, I'm glad you're going. I get it. But you'll be back.

DAVID. Take my un-legal advice and go. I don't know what's out there or where there is to go anymore. But do it.

DOROTHY. I'm going to take your advice and go too, David. Don't get up. I'm used to going home alone. I may even prefer it. Good night, Johnny. Or should I say Bon Voyage?

*(**DOROTHY** exits.)*

JOHNNY. I didn't know things were so bad.

DAVID. We should have been better friends, Johnny.

JOHNNY. We had big dreams, didn't we?

DAVID. Yes. And too many of them came true. Damn it.

(**LORRAINE** *enters.*)

[MUSIC NO. 12A "COCKTAIL MUSIC"]

LORRAINE. Johnny, I'd like to talk to David.

DAVID. I don't blame you if you're angry.

LORRAINE. That's very considerate of you.

DAVID. I know this has been awkward tonight.

LORRAINE. Awkward? Is that all you have to say to me?

DAVID. Johnny invited her this afternoon. I couldn't call you.

LORRAINE. I know. He told me.

DAVID. Then you're not angry?

LORRAINE. I love you, David. But when I saw you sitting at our table with her...

DAVID. I know.

LORRAINE. No, you don't know. You'll never know how I felt. She's much different than I expected. She's pretty... in a mature way.

DAVID. Let's not talk about her.

LORRAINE. She wants a divorce, David.

DAVID. I don't want to talk about her.

LORRAINE. Well, we can't talk about us without talking about her and I want to talk about us! David, we can't sneak around anymore. Do you know, I don't think I've ever seen you in the daylight.

DAVID. I don't know what to do.

(*"Cocktail Music" fades out.*)

LORRAINE. Make a move. She wants a divorce. Johnny is closing the playground.

DAVID. You could reconsider my offer.

LORRAINE. I will not be set up in an apartment.

DAVID. If we had a place I'd be with you whenever I could.

LORRAINE. What about the rest of the time?

[MUSIC NO. 13 "QUIET, INTIMATE LITTLE RESTAURANTS"]

ROSIE.

WE MEET IN QUIET, INTIMATE LITTE RESTAURANTS
REMINISCENT OF THE RENAISSANCE.
LOUSY FOOD, BUT LOTS OF AMBIENCE.
WE CAN'T GO ON MEETING LIKE THIS.
CRAMMED IN NOOKS, WATCHING CALORIES.
KNOWING LOOKS IN EAST SIDE GALLERIES.
THROWING HOOKS IN BOWLING ALLERIES.
WE CAN'T GO ON MEETING LIKE THIS.

FIXING ICE AND MIXING DRINKS
IN WAITING ROOMS AND SKATING RINKS.
UNDER VEILS, HAGS AND BITCHES.
COUTURE THAT GOES FROM RAGS TO RICHES—

YOU AND I ARE VERY ILL AT EASE
PLAYING AT RESPECTABILITY.
GONE IS THE THRILL, COMES THE SENILITY
MUCH TOO EARLY...

TIDY SUMS I SPEND ON BENZEDRINES.
HIDING FROM RELENTLESS MAGAZINES.
RIDING DUMB IN RENTED LIMOUSINES.
WE CAN'T GO ON MEETING LIKE THIS.

ENDLESS APOLOGIES, FUMBLED PASSES.
ALWAYS YOU IN THOSE DAMNED DARK GLASSES.
IN DISGUISE FROM HEAD TO FEET OH,
MUST WE BE SO INCOGNITO?

CRACKING LOBSTER SOMEWHERE BY THE SEA.
MILES OUT, BUT AH THE PRIVACY.
SECRET FEES YOU SLIP THE DRIVERS
MAÎTRE DS ACCEPTING FIVERS.
IN MY SOUL I'VE STORED A RIOT.
I'M SO SICK OF PEACE AND QUIIIIII—

ROSIE.

> —ET INTIMATE LITTLE RESTAURANTS
> REMINISCENT OF THE RENAISSANCE.
> LOUSY FOOD, BUT LOTS OF AMBIENCE.
> WE CAN'T GO ON MEETING LIKE,
> WE CAN'T GO ON EATING LIKE,
> WE CAN'T GO ON MEETING LIKE THIS!

> *(***DOROTHY*** re-enters and catches **LORRAINE** and **DAVID** together. **DAVID** panics.)*

DOROTHY. Sit down, David. *(To* **LORRAINE.***)* Look, I don't know who you are...

But I do know you're type.

LORRAINE. Look, Dorothy...

DOROTHY. Don't "Look, Dorothy" me. I am Mrs. Darling to you. Mrs. David Darling. So this is where you've been spending your time. Johnny, you run a very interesting business here.

DAVID. This is all my fault. Don't blame Johnny.

LORRAINE. This is our chance. She gets a divorce. You get your freedom and...

DOROTHY. And you get the biggest headache you've ever had. Now there are two immediate courses of action. I can either blow the roof off this place. Or I can be terribly sophisticated. And I *can* be terribly sophisticated. I think I'll go to the bar and mull all this over. Why don't you two do whatever it is you two do together. You know what the real shame is, David?

DAVID. What?

DOROTHY. I am going to sue the pants off you. And you're my lawyer. Sit down, David.

RITA. *(Feeling the champagne.)* People don't know how to act in public anymore.

[MUSIC CUE 13A "COCKTAIL MUSIC"]

MICKEY. Were you really on the Titanic?

RITA. What kind of question is that? You are evil! You don't seem to know who you're talking to.

MICKEY. No. I guess I don't. If you were so famous and such a big star how come I never heard of you?

RITA. You never heard of me because the world forgets. Fast. You wait. I had a following then...a public. The critics loved me.

MICKEY. Well, that was then and this is now. For an old lady, you got a lot to learn.

RITA. I am *not* an old lady. I *know* old ladies and as a matter of fact most of the old ladies I know are men. *(Aside.)* I think I married one. As for you, my boy, you have just talked yourself out of a sizable tip. Now please, go away.

MICKEY. Whatever you say, Rita.

(**MICKEY** *goes to the bar.*)

RITA. *(To* **GARY.***)* More champagne!

DOROTHY. Do you mind if I say something?

MICKEY. No, what.

DOROTHY. Hello.

MICKEY. Hello.

ROSIE. Well, Johnny, you've really done it tonight. You pulled the rug out.

JOHNNY. People should be used to that by now living in this city.

ROSIE. You have everything you want here... Johnny Manhattan's...

JOHNNY. Even the name is phony. A nightclub is not what I want. I thought it was. But it's not for every day of the year. It's not for Christmas.

ROSIE. We had good Christmases, Johnny.

JOHNNY. It wasn't enough, Rosie.

ROSIE. Nothing's ever enough for you, Johnny.

JOHNNY. You know what I miss most? Fighting with you.

ROSIE. Johnny.

JOHNNY. Making up with you. Making love. Racing the sunrise.

ROSIE. STOP IT, Johnny! I know what you're doing. Twisting everything so I'll feel sorry for you. You gave up on us. You gave up on ME. So you're leaving? Fine. Terrific. Only I'm leaving first this time.

JOHNNY. Rosie!

ROSIE. And when you finally come back, and I know you will, there just might not be anything left to come back to.

*(**ROSIE** gets her coat and exits.)*

RITA. Where's my champagne?

*(**PAUL** brings more champagne. Light on **RITA** only.)*

I'm not an old lady. *(Pause.)* Where does the time go? I had a following. Fan letters. People I'd never even met would write and say the sweetest things. And oh God, how I loved the war. We all stood together then. We thought we knew who the enemy was.

[MUSIC NO. 14 "OH THOSE JOHNNIES"]

Everybody had a good time. I had a public. I had a private, too. First Class! His name was Johnny.

*(This is all internal for **RITA** so it's not a song anyone else hears.)*

(Tentatively.) OH THOSE JOHNNIES, OH THOSE
  JOHNNIES.
THANK YOU FOR BREAKING YOUR NECKS.
MARCH HOME AND IF YOU CANNOT MARCH.
CRAWL HOME AND IF YOU CANNOT CRAWL,
ASK THEM TO SEND YOU...

OH THOSE JOHNNIES, SO YOUNG THOSE JOHNNIES.
NOT KNOWING WHAT TO EXPECT.
MARCH HOME AND IF YOU CANNOT MARCH.
CRAWL HOME AND IF YOU CANNOT CRAWL,
ASK THEM TO SEND YOU COLLECT!

HE ONLY HAD A WEEK
SO WE ONLY HAD A WEEK

AND WE HARDLY EVER FOUND THE TIME TO SPEAK.
HE WAS SOMETHING OR OTHER
I GUESS YOU'D SAY MY LOVER
AND I DID NOT PAINT MY FACE ONCE THAT WHOLE WEEK.
HE SANG ME A SONG.
SANG IT JUST FOR ME.
HE SANG IT OUT STRONG
THOUGH HE SANG IT OFF KEY.
HE SANG IT ALL WRONG
RIGHT FROM THE START
AND TO THIS DAY, JOHNNY.
IT BREAKS MY HEART.
I CALLED HIM JOHNNY... JOHNNY,
AND I LET HIM TAKE ME OFF MY LITTLE SHELF.
I CALLED HIM JOHNNY... JOHNNY,
AND I DON'T REMEMBER WHAT I CALLED MYSELF.
JOHNNY, JOHNNY, ALL NIGHT THROUGH.
EVERYTHING REMINDS ME OF YOU.

HE WAS HERE FOR A WHILE IF A WEEK IS A WHILE
AND I ALWAYS CALLED HIM JOHNNY, NEVER JACK.
HE WAS SOMETHING OR OTHER
I GUESS YOU'D SAY MY LOVER
AND I USED TO THINK THAT HE WAS COMING BACK.

HE MADE ME SING.
HE BOUGHT ME A RING.
I TELL YOU THAT RING,
IT WAS THE PRETTIEST THING.
IT WAS THE PRETTIEST RING
I'D EVER SEEN.
AND TO THIS DAY, JOHNNY,
MY FINGER'S GREEN!

I CALLED HIM JOHNNY... JOHNNY,
AND HE USED TO LOVE TO WATCH ME BRUSH MY HAIR.
I CALLED HIM JOHNNY... JOHNNY,
AND HOW I LOVED TO WATCH HIM LYING THERE.

JOHNNY, JOHNNY, ALL NIGHT THROUGH,
EVERYTHING REMINDS ME OF

RITA.

> ALL THOSE JOHNNIES. OH, THOSE JOHNNIES.
> NOT KNOWING WHAT TO EXPECT.
> MARCH HOME AND IF YOU CANNOT MARCH.
> CRAWL HOME AND IF YOU CANNOT CRAWL,
> ASK THEM TO SEND YOU CO—
>
> OH MY JOHNNY, SO YOUNG MY JOHNNY.
> I NEVER KNEW WHAT TO EXPECT.
> MARCH HOME AND IF YOU CANNOT MARCH.
> CRAWL HOME AND IF YOU CANNOT CRAWL,
> ASK THEM TO SEND YOU,
> ASK THEM TO SEND YOU,
> ASK THEM TO SEND YOU
> COLLECT!

JOHNNY. You'd better sit down, Rita.

RITA. I'm alright. A little bit too much champagne over the dam I guess.

JOHNNY. I have to talk to you.

RITA. Not now. Please, not now.

JOHNNY. He was my father wasn't he?

RITA. Who?

JOHNNY. Johnny. Your Johnny was my father.

RITA. Yes. I always wanted to tell you about him.

JOHNNY. Well, it's hard to talk to someone when you're not there.

RITA. I wanted to be there. But what could I do? I left you in good hands. I saw you when I could. I thought about you all the time.

JOHNNY. I wanted to be your son in real life.

RITA. Please don't Johnny. I was just a kid. I would have been a terrible mother. You can get away with having an illegitimate child nowadays but you couldn't back then. And I had my career, such as it was, the party that wasn't supposed to end. You look so much like him.

JOHNNY. Who was he? I'm leaving. I want to know.

RITA. Promise me you'll never ask me again. *(JOHNNY nods yes.)* He was a soldier, just like you were. And I had only been in New York for a short time. I was on my way somewhere... And this soldier stopped to ask me for directions. He was on a week's leave. We ended up spending that whole day together. Well, he never got where he was going either. He was the first man I ever really loved. He wasn't a sophisticated man. He was rather coarse. But he had his soft spots. And they were so soft. He said, "I love you" to me every day we were together. I never knew when to expect it. I never did expect it. But it was the kind of "I love you" that stopped me dead in my tracks no matter what I was doing. Seven days. Seven "I love yous." He died three months after that. I read about it. A list in the paper.

JOHNNY. Can't we just tell everyone? Get it out in the open?

RITA. How old are you Johnny?

JOHNNY. Forty-fo—

RITA. Don't even say it because by my calculations I would have been about nine when you were born. And nobody's gonna believe that. I went away. Now *you're* going away. Well, I guess that's good, if that's what you need. But let me tell you something, Johnny. For what it's worth, I love you. Now do me one big favor.

JOHNNY. What?

RITA. Call me Rita.

> *(Scene shifts to* DOROTHY *and* MICKEY *at the bar.)*

[MUSIC NO. 14A "COCKTAIL MUSIC"]

DOROTHY. Do you think of me as an older woman?

MICKEY. No. Do you think of me as a younger man?

DOROTHY. Yes. Are you very expensive?

MICKEY. Yes.

DOROTHY. Good. *(Indicating* DAVID.) He can afford it.

(Shift to **DAVID** *and* **LORRAINE** *at the table.)*

LORRAINE. Let's go to a hotel tonight.

DAVID. We're not leaving until she does. *(Indicating* **DOROTHY.***)*

FRANCINE. *(To* **EDWARD.***)* C'mon let's dance.

EDWARD. I think I'll sit this one out.

FRANCINE. C'mon.

*(***FRANCINE** *and* **GLORIA** *drag him onstage.)*

EDWARD. No, I'd rather not.

GLORIA. It won't hurt.

EDWARD. I'm not so sure.

FRANCINE. We may not get this chance again.

EDWARD. You're very sweet. You know I used to look forward to all the things I was going to do. Then one day I overheard myself talking about all the things I used to do...when I was younger.

[MUSIC NO. 15 "I DON'T DO THAT ANYMORE"]

I USED TO SING SONGS, LA DA DA DE DUM.
SOMETIMES I'D WHISTLE, SOMETIMES I'D HUM.
I'D SING LIKE A BIRD AND LET THE RAIN POUR,
BUT I DON'T DO THAT ANYMORE.
I USED TO TAKE WALKS IN THE PARK.
AFTERNOONS OR AFTER DARK.

FREE AS A BIRD, NO LOCK ON THE DOOR.
BUT I DON'T DO THAT ANYMORE.

I USED TO DANCE. CAN YOU IMAGINE THAT?
I WAS READY FOR ROMANCE AT THE DROP OF A HAT
OR A SHOE OR A HINT OR TWO.
I USED TO LAUGH. CAN YOU IMAGINE THAT?
NEW YORK TOWN, WHERE'S THE THRILL?
IF THE AIR DOESN'T GET YOU, THE ENNUI WILL!
I USED TO TELL JOKES. I USED TO HAVE FUN.
I HAD A GOOD WORD FOR EV'RYONE.

LAUGHED LIKE A KID IN A CANDY STORE.
BUT I DON'T DO THAT ANYMORE.

I'D BE SO SMOOTH. NEAT AS A PIN.
GIRLS WOULD SWOON WHEN I WALKED IN.
LIGHT AS A EATHER. FREE AS A BIRD.
EXCUSE ME FOR ASKING, BUT HAVEN'T YOU HEARD?
I DON'T DO THAT ANYMORE.

    (Dance break.)

I USED TO TAKE WALKS DOWN BROADWAY.
WE DID THOSE CAKEWALKS. *(TO* **RITA***.)*
HEY DON'T YOU REMEMBER?
WE FOLLOWED THE BEAT OF A RATATATAT DRUM,
I USED TO SING SONGS, LA DA DA DA DUM.
BUT I DON'T DO THAT ANYMORE.

RITA. Edward, you're an old fool. *(To* **JOHNNY***.)* You're sitting in the man's seat. *(To* **EDWARD***.)* Sit down before you have a heart attack.

    (Scene shifts to bar.)

MICKEY. Hey, [Pianist's name]. How 'bout a rhumba?

[MUSIC NO. 15A "COCKTAIL MUSIC"]

DOROTHY. Do you think you could teach me how to have fun?

MICKEY. That's my specialty.

DOROTHY. You're very sure of yourself aren't you?

MICKEY. I'm not sure of anything.

DOROTHY. No, I didn't think so.

MICKEY. Would you like me to take you home?

DOROTHY. We're not leaving until he *(Indicating* **DAVID***.)* does.

MAXIE. Okay, sit down everybody. I *said* sit down!

    ("Cocktail Music" ends abruptly.)

It's Maxie's turn for a change. Don't try to stop me Johnny.

MAXIE. Here, hand these out. *(She gives the pianist the orchestra parts.)* Since I might be looking for another job tomorrow anyway, I thought I'd like to tell you all a little story. It's about me. It's called "Maxie." Or "How to be an Overnight Sensation in Just thirty Short Years." A comedy.

(**MAXIE** *cues the pianist.*)

[MUSIC NO. 16 "MISTER PRODUCER"]

WHEN I LEFT MY LITTLE HOME IN CALIFORNIA,
MY FOLKS BOTH SAID, GOOD-BYE AND PLEASE DON'T
    WRITE."
THEN I BOARDED A GREYHOUND, MY BEAUTIFUL
    BROADWAY BOUND
BUS, AND TRAVELED THROUGH THE NIGHT.

And day and night and God, it took forever.

I REMEMBER FIRST ARRIVING IN THE CITY.
IT WAS THRILLING. I FELT LIKE I HAD WINGS.
I BENT DOWN TO KISS THE GROUND AND WHEN I
    TURNED AROUND
SOMEONE HAD STOLEN ALL MY THINGS.

I also got an infection on my lip. But, no matter. I was here and I was gonna make it!

SOON AFTER THAT I GOT MY FIRST AUDITION.
I WAS SCARED, I WAS NERVOUS, I WAS TENSE.
MY HEART DID A FRANTIC JIG WHEN I SPOTTED "MISTER
    BIG"
SITTING IN THE AUDIENCE.

It was then I knew it was him or me!

SO I MUSTERED ALL THE CHARM THEY HAD INSTILLED
    AT THE CONSERVATORY
THIS WAS SURE TO BE A THEATRICAL EVENT.
IF YOU WANT A TALE OF GLORY, JUST RELAX, 'CAUSE
    HERE'S THE STORY.
HERE'S EXACTLY HOW IT WENT.

MISTER PRODUCER, HOW DO YOU DO, SIR?
PLEASE TO MEET YOU, SIR, TODAY.
FRESH FROM THE CLOSET HERE'S MY COMPOSITE
AND HERE'S MY RÉSUMÉ.

NOW, HOW'D YA LIKE TO HEAR MY OBLIGATO? HA!
HOW'D YA LIKE TO SEE ME WORK ON POINTE?
WHEN I SANG AIDA, THE FAMILY AGREED, A –
DORABLE AND I LIT UP THE JOINT!
(JUST AN EXPRESSION.)

HOW'D YA LIKE TO SEE MY DESDEMONA?
HOW'S ABOUT A BIT OF JULIET? ROMEO, ROMEO.
THE COMMUNITY THEATRE SAID NO ONE'S DONE IT
    GREATER.
WAIT, I HAVEN'T DONE THE GOOD PART YET...

What? I need experience? On the road? What road?
Oh, that road!

GARY, PAUL & GEORGE. One year later!

MAXIE.

MISTER PRODUCER, WELL, HOW DO YOU DO, SIR?
ALWAYS NICE TO SEE YOU, SIR. IT'S GREAT!
THIS TIME I'M HOPING I'LL CLICK, SIR
YOU'VE ALREADY GOT MY PICTURE.
HERE'S MY RÉSUMÉ UP TO DATE.

NOW, HOW'D YA LIKE TO HEAR ME BELT A NUMBER?
HOW'D YA LIKE TO SEE MY ROUTINE?
I TWIRL A BATON WITH VERY LITTLE ON
THEN I DO THIS BIT WITH GASOLINE... IT'S HILARIOUS.

HOW'D YA LIKE TO SEE MY DESDEMONA?
HOW'S ABOUT A BIT OF JULIET? ROMEO, ROMEO.
THE FOLKS BACK IN COLUSA SAY "SHE'S ANOTHER DUSE."
WAIT, YOU HAVEN' HEARD MY OBLIGATO YET.
    AAAAAAAAHHH!

What?! I need more experience! But sir, I've been on
the road for a year already! Another year? ...

GARY, PAUL & GEORGE. One year later!

MAXIE.

MR. PRODUCER, YEAH, HOW DO YOU DO, SIR?
I'VE GOT SOMETHING FOR YOU, SIR, THAT'S HOT.
I'M MORE THAN A CUT-UP, SO PLEASE SIT DOWN AND
    SHUT UP
AND LET ME SHOW YA WHAT I'VE GOT.

OH, OH, OH... HOW'D YA LIKE TO SEE A LITTLE GLAMOUR?
HOW'D YA LIKE TO SEE A LITTLE GLITZ?
WHEN I DO MY STUFF THOSE HICKS CAN'T GET ENOUGH.
NOW, HOW'D YA LIKE TO SEE MY...
HOW'D YA LIKE TO HEAR MY OBLIGATO?
HOW'S ABOUT A GANDER AT MY LEGS?
PERHAPS YOU'D LIKE MY NECK BEST?
HOW'D YA LIKE TO STAY FOR BREAKFAST?
HOW'D YA LIKE TO HAVE YOUR EGGS? ...IN THE MORNING.

HOW'D YA LIKE TO SEE MY DESDEMONA?
HOW'S ABOUT A PIECE OF JULIET? ROMEO!!
HAD YOUR DINNER YET? WHY NOT START WITH JULIET?
WAIT! YOU HAVEN'T HAD YOUR DESDEMONA...

WHAT??!!

You're looking for new faces?!! Don't you "old-timer me!"

MISTER PRODUCER, YEAH, I'M TALKING TO YOU SIR,
TELL ME, WHERE DO YOU GET YOUR BRASS?
I'M SICK OF THIS CRAP, YOU CAN TAKE THE BIG APPLE
    AND
SHOVE IT UP YOUR...

AS FOR THE FUTURE WHAT I WANNA KNOW IS
WHERE'S MR. ZIEGFELD? WHERE ARE YA, FLO?
TWO LONG YEARS ON THAT DAMNED BUS
AND ALL I EVER GET IS, "DON'T CALL US."

MISTER PRODUCER, WHAT I WANNA KNOW IS
WHERE DID ALL THE GOOD GUYS GO?
WHERE DID ALL THE GOOD GUYS GO?

[MUSIC NO. 16A "PLAYOFF"]
[MUSIC NO. 16B: "COCKTAIL MUSIC"]

(**MAXIE** *runs off to the dressing room.*)

(*In the following scene* **DAVID** *and* **LORRAINE** *are dancing and* **DOROTHY** *and* **MICKEY** *are dancing in a different area.*)

DOROTHY. What do you suppose he wants?

MICKEY. It's hard to say.

DOROTHY. What do you want?

MICKEY. Me? I want everything.

DOROTHY. Good for you. I like to travel. I'm sure you do too.

LORRAINE. We'll get married now, won't we?

DAVID. Yes. I – uh –

LORRAINE. What?

DAVID. Well, all of a sudden there are a lot of loose ends. Things to be taken care of. I want you to be happy.

LORRAINE. I want you, David.

DOROTHY. There are so many places I've never seen.

MICKEY. Egypt. Let's go there.

DOROTHY. Yes. I'd like that. There are places I'd like to return to.

LORRAINE. Can we have a honeymoon?

DOROTHY. The boys would stay here, of course.

DAVID. She'll probably want custody of the children.

LORRAINE. That's all right.

MICKEY. I don't really like kids. Never have.

LORRAINE. I think I'd get depressed having people that much younger than me around all the time.

DOROTHY. There's a restaurant in Juan-les-Pins. It's built on a pier over the Mediterranean.

DAVID. A honeymoon. Yes. I'd like that.

DOROTHY. We can dance there all night if we want.

DAVID. We can watch the lights on the water. You'll wear that soft blue dress.

DOROTHY. I'll do something with my hair. We'll be the only Americans.

DAVID. We'll make plans. Do you like children?

DOROTHY. We have a lot in common.

DAVID. The same dreams.

DOROTHY. For better or for worse.

DAVID. Yes, yes. I'll marry you. It'll be a good life, Dorothy.

LORRAINE. David, I'm not Dorothy.

[MUSIC NO. 17 "AND I WOULD GO AWAY / EVERY NOW AND THEN"]

DOROTHY.

AND I WOULD GO AWAY,
BUT WHO WOULD KEEP THE CHILDREN WARM,
SAFE FROM HARM AND FROM THE STORM
AND WHO'D ARRANGE THE ROSES?
AND I WOULD GO AWAY,
BUT WHO WOULD FEEL THE EMPTY STROKES,
LAUGH AT ALL HIS FOOLISH JOKES,
AND WHO WOULD BUY THE PAPER?

AND I WOULD GO TO SINGAPORE TO HIDE,
I HAVE FRIENDS IN FLORENCE... WELL, REALLY JUST
    OUTSIDE.
A STRANGER IN A RAINCOAT, A MYST'RY IN A HAT.
AND I WOULD GO TO ZANZIBAR... ZANZIBAR? WHERE'S
    THAT?

AND I WOULD GO AWAY
FROM CROSSWORD-PUZZLED SUNDAY MORN,
BUT WHO WOULD KEEP
STANDING IN MY WAY
AND WHERE WOULD I GO?

AND I WOULD GO AWAY
FROM ROSES, CHILDREN, STORM AND SNOW
BUT HOW COULD I GO?
YOU'RE STANDING IN MY WAY.
AND WHERE WOULD I GO?

DAVID.

> EVERY NOW AND THEN,
> I NEVER KNOW JUST WHEN,
> THERE COMES A CERTAIN EV'NING
> WHEN THERE'S SOMETHING IN THE AIR.
> TIME FOR REMEMBERING WHO WE WERE
> AND WHAT WE WERE AND WHERE.
>
> AND WHENEVER THE MUSIC IS SLOW
> AND MORE ROMANTIC THAN SUITS MY TASTE...
> THERE IT GOES AGAIN.
> IT TAKES ME AWAY AND I THINK ABOUT THE GIRL
> LONG AGO, FAR AWAY.
> HAIR WAS SO MUCH SOFTER THEN AND PROMISES...
>
> I CAN'T RECALL YOUR NAME.
> THANK YOU ALL THE SAME.
> I WON'T RECALL YOUR NAME,
> BUT THANK YOU FOR THAT SPECIAL EV'NING.
> SOMETHING IN THE AIR.
> TIME FOR REMEMBERING
> WHO WE ARE, AND WHAT WE ARE, AND WHERE...

> > (**DAVID** and **DOROTHY** *sing from opposite sides of the room.*)

DAVID & DOROTHY.

> AND I WOULD GO AWAY
> FROM ROSES, CHILDREN, STORM, AND SNOW,
> BUT HOW COULD I GO?
> YOU'RE STANDING IN MY WAY.
> AND WHERE WOULD I GO?

DOROTHY. *(To* **DAVID.***)* I'll get our coats. *(To* **LORRAINE.***)* I'm sorry. This isn't the first time this has happened.

LORRAINE. Good-bye, David.

MICKEY. C'mon Lorraine. I'll walk you home.

LORRAINE. Thanks.

> > (**LORRAINE** *and* **MICKEY** *exit.*)

RITA. Edward.

EDWARD. Well, Rita, it's been quite a night. This is one for the memoirs.

RITA. Edward, that's it.

EDWARD. What?

RITA. You'll help me write my memoirs. I've been waiting for the right time. We'll make a fortune.

EDWARD. I can't do it.

RITA. Why not?

EDWARD. I can't write anymore. I have nothing to say.

RITA. Well, I do. Look, you say you're not as young as you used to be. Well, I'm not as old as I used to be. Survival. That's the game. And we're old hands, Edward. Keep your eyes open or they'll send you to Florida.

EDWARD. Memoirs?

RITA. C'mon, Edward.

EDWARD. We could call it "RITA"!

RITA. Or, "Where Did the Time Go?"

EDWARD. We'll start at the present and work our way backwards. Riches to rags.

RITA. Rags to rags. I'm dead broke, you know.

EDWARD. You too?

RITA. Have been for years. (**EDWARD** *laughs.*)
The only thing left is this chinchilla. And I'm seriously thinking of donating it to the Museum of Natural History.

EDWARD. "Rita".

RITA. I can see it now.

EDWARD. We'll do an individual profile on each of your husbands.

RITA. That's enough material for an encyclopedia.

EDWARD. We'll tell everything?

RITA. Everything I can remember. The rest we'll make up. Ah, we'll travel first class again, Edward. Do you have money for a cab?

EDWARD. No.

RITA. Then we'll walk first class. *(They start to exit.)*
Oh my God. I almost forgot the baby. *(She gets the chinchilla.)* Goodnight, Johnny. And forget everything I ever told you.

> *(RITA and EDWARD exit.)*

MAXIE. We all decided we're coming in tomorrow night anyway, Johnny. Just in case you change your mind about leaving.

> *(MAXIE starts crying.)*

JOHNNY. Thanks, Maxie. You'll be alright.

GLORIA. Maxie, I've never seen you cry before. Johnny's right, you'll be alright.

FRANCINE. We'll all be alright.

JOHNNY. Good night, kids.

> *(STAFF, except GARY exits saying goodnight. One waiter says "It's not good-bye.")*

Get home safe.

MAXIE. *(Running back in.)* Johnny, You can't walk away from a good time.

GLORIA. Come on, Maxie.

> *(The pianist shakes hands with JOHNNY and exits.)*

JOHNNY. Gary, it's time to go home.

GARY. Alright, boss. I'll be here tomorrow.

> *(GARY exits as ROSIE enters.)*

ROSIE. Well Johnny, like they say—the party's over.

JOHNNY. I keep hearing your voice, Rosie. I thought you left.

ROSIE. I did.

JOHNNY. She's my mother, Rosie.

ROSIE. Maxie is your mother?

JOHNNY. No. Rita.

ROSIE. Somehow, that makes sense. So, what's the problem?

JOHNNY. I'm not her son. Not to the world.

ROSIE. Ah, the world. What do they know? Do you love her?

JOHNNY. Yes.

ROSIE. She love you?

JOHNNY. Yes.

ROSIE. Sounds good to me, Johnny. Now you're gonna walk out on all these people. They need you. That's what scares you doesn't it?

JOHNNY. I need them. That's what scares me.

ROSIE. Come home with me...for the night.

JOHNNY. It's nearly dawn.

ROSIE. Perfect. We'll race the sunrise.

JOHNNY. We lost that race a long time ago. Don't you remember how we treated one another at the end of it.

ROSIE. I remember how it was at the beginning.

JOHNNY. Get yourself a new race, Rosie. You deserve that.

ROSIE. I deserve you.

JOHNNY. I'm no good.

ROSIE. I know that. C'mon Johnny. For me? For you? For Johnny Manhattan's?

[MUSIC NO. 18 "FOR OLD TIMES' SAKE – REPRISE"]

FOR OLD TIMES' SAKE, LET'S TAKE
ONE MORE CHANCE IN MANHATTAN,
ONE MORE CHANCE IN NEW YORK.
ONE MORE RIVER OF CHAMPAGNE,
ALL THOSE BOTTLES TO UNCORK.

BOTH.

ONE MORE CHANCE IN THE CITY,
ONE MORE CHANCE TO GET A BREAK,
AND A RIVER OF CHAMPAGNE
TO MAKE IT EASIER TO TAKE

JOHNNY.
>WILL LOVE LAST OR WILL IT DIE?
>IS THERE MUCH TOO MUCH AT STAKE?

ROSIE.
>LET'S GIVE IT ONE MORE TRY
>FOR OLD TIMES' SAKE.

JOHNNY.
>FOR OLD TIMES' SAKE

ROSIE.
>THERE'S A MORNING TO BE FACED,
>A SUNRISE TO BE RACED,

JOHNNY.
>A RAINBOW TO BE CHASED ACROSS THE SKY.

ROSIE.
>TURN OUT ALL THE LIGHTS
>GIVE MY ACHING BACK A BREAK.

JOHNNY. I don't know if I've got the guts for this, Rosie.

ROSIE.
>WELL, PRETEND THAT YOU DO
>FOR OLD TIMES' SAKE.

BOTH.
>FOR OLD TIMES' SAKE.

[MUSIC NO. 19 "BOWS"]

End of Play

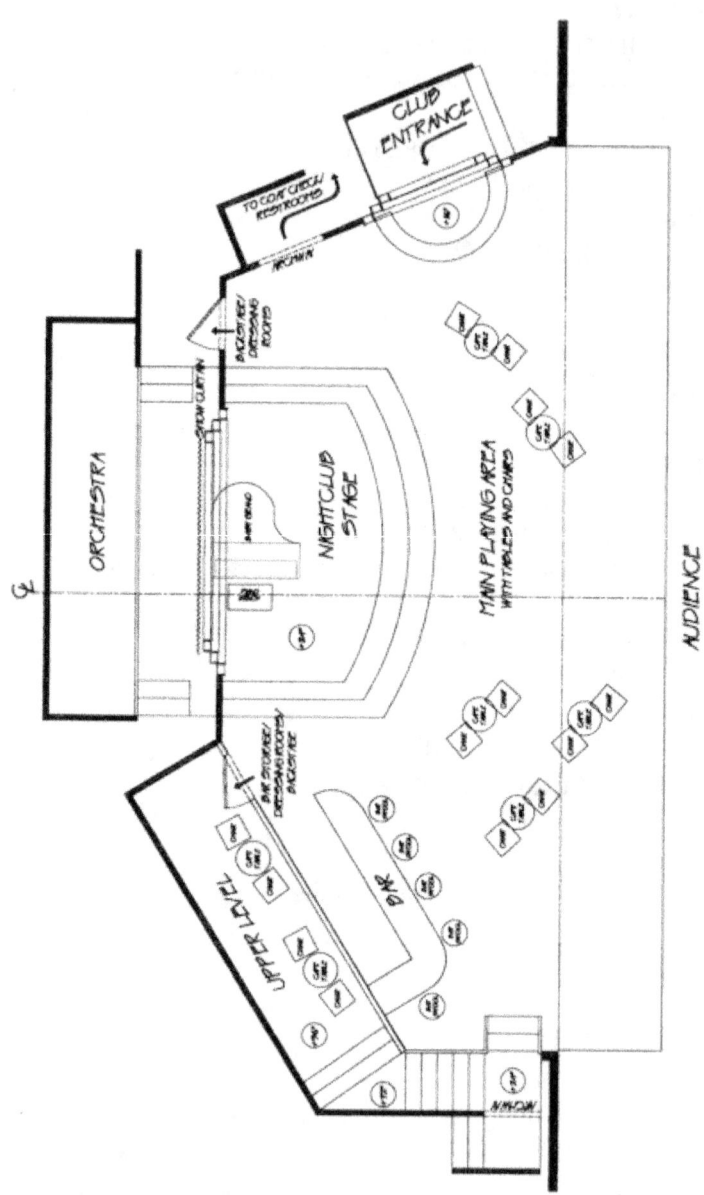

Set and Ground Plan
Designed and Built by Brian Kessler